A Cromer Co

A CROMER CORPSE

Kelvin I. Jones

CUNNING CRIME BOOKS

A Cromer Corpse

First published as an ebook in 2011
This edition published 2015

A Cromer Corpse

CHAPTER ONE

He saw it as the net was slowly winched up onto the trawler deck: a white, bloated thing which had lain in the waves for three weeks, a thing like a tailor's dummy, the arms and legs rigid and attenuated, the head a misshapen doll's face, one of the eyes eaten away, the mouth still bloody and wide open. Around the body, fish struggled and squirmed, as if trying to free themselves from this hideous relic of the deep.

As the jib swung across to meet him, Zak smelt it too, the charnel house odour of decaying flesh. He jerked back, gripped by nausea, releasing the control arm. The jib lurched above him, the net slipping with the recoil, jettisoning its grotesque trophy onto the deck where it stared back at him with malevolent intent.

* * *

Bottrell saw the layby and the country park sign, turned the wheel of the Skoda and parked it between the lorries. He opened the car door. The heat him like a furnace. All that day the sun had beaten down on him remorselessly, from the moment he had set out from the Lizard peninsula. For each of the 300 miles he had sat in the driver's seat, sweat trickling down his neck. Even with all the windows open it had made little difference.

He locked the car, made his way slowly over to the catering cabin, downed a cold drink, then sought shade under a row of tall pine trees. The air was cooler here and a slight breeze shifted the heat from his face. He wiped his forehead and neck, finished his drink, then lay

A Cromer Corpse

back on the sandy bank and closed his eyes for a moment. A kaleidoscope of images burned his retinae: the cottage in St Sampson, Melanie's face, the narrow country lanes of West Cornwall and the broad flat lands of East Anglia.

It had been almost a year since the St Sampson murders. Although his injuries had healed he still experienced nightmares about what had happened. Melanie had come close to death and her daughter had died at the hands of a vicious psychopath. Unable to come to terms with the memory of those traumatic events, she had put the cottage up for sale and moved here to Norfolk, partly to be nearer to her aged mother but also to make a fresh start. For some weeks, Bottrell had lingered on in St Sampson, unsure of what next to do. The county still held memories of his dead wife Frances and he felt that leaving Cornwall might amount to some sort of betrayal. But in the end his attachment to Melanie got the better of him. He put his cottage up for sale and set out on the trek eastwards.

The night before he had left he had taken the car down to the Lizard and sat on the headland, watching the sun slowly set on a still and almost motionless sea. Only the mournful cries of gulls disturbed his reverie. Out here on the headland, surrounded by the barrows and remains of vanished iron age peoples, he felt utterly alone, yet strangely comforted.

He finished his drink, then got back into the car. The catering van was busy with tourists now and the sickly smell of fried burgers hung heavy on the warm, still air. He drove on, past avenues of tall pine trees until the road ran alongside the long border fence of Lakenheath air base. Here a small group of dishevelled peace protesters gathered around a couple of makeshift benders. He

A Cromer Corpse

grinned at them and sounded his horn, recalling his own days in the '70s as a CND supporter. An old man with a white beard waved back at him.

The car moved on, through scattered red-brick villages and past broad fields, bearing the sickly smell of oil seed rape, until at last he found himself in a long tail back on the outskirts of Fakenham. He sat in the sweltering heat, smelling car exhaust, watching the sun burn the grimy streets. He glanced down at the passenger seat where Melanie's letter and the photo of Lodge House lay across the open road atlas. The photo was of a small Elizabethan style house with a flat brick front and mullioned windows and dormers with pinnacles. Outside the front door stood Melanie. She was dressed in a light cotton dress and in her arms was Grimalkin, the large white cat Bottrell had grown so fond of during his early days at the cottage in Cornwall. She was standing in a relaxed pose, the late afternoon sun reflecting on her blonde hair and on the leaded windows behind her. Though marked by the tragedy of her daughter's death, Melanie still retained a lightness of spirit which served as a lesson to Bottrell, a melancholic who had never quite come to terms with his wife's death.

Melanie had taught him to laugh again and also she had another gift. Like Bottrell, she understood the power of the numinous. It occurred to him, as the rows of cars ahead began slowly to move, that their discovery of each other had been no mere coincidence. He also had the power to look between worlds, a surprising ability considering his former vocation as a detective, yet one which had often served him well in difficult situations during his years in the Met.

He was travelling due north now on a winding B road. Passing a series of scattered hamlets with solid Saxon

A Cromer Corpse

names like Warham and Wighton, he soon hit the A road which clung to the coast where his route took him past Wells, Stiffkey and Blakeney. The air here was clearer and with the car windows down, he could smell the salt North sea. He turned the car radio on and put on a Rolling Stones track. The music, the open spaces and the anticipation of seeing Melanie again combined to raise his spirits. Then, a mile onwards, he passed the long, low spit of Morton with its great sand dunes and marshes.

He took a sharp right turn, catching a brief glimpse of Morton Wood to his right. Then he saw it: the roof of Hautbois Lodge with its red brick polygonal chimneys. He had arrived at last. This was to be his new home.

* * *

"So he drowned, then ?" asked an exasperated Charles Grayling. Although DCI Grayling had known Max Cameron for the last seven years, he had never quite got used to his infuriating method. It was a method which resembled an annoying game in which Grayling would ask a number of questions for which only partial answers would be provided in replies such as "maybe", or "not quite", or "you're almost correct but not entirely." Cameron was exasperating, there was no doubt about it. And it was not just with Grayling he played the game. He did it with everyone, hence the popular epithet: "cussid Cameron."

"Not entirely, though in a sense you're correct," came the laconic reply.

"For God's sake, Cameron, did he drown or didn't he ?" exploded Grayling.

A Cromer Corpse

It had been a long and tiring day. The fishing vessel off Cromer which had alerted the authorities, had docked at 6am. The rest of the morning had been spent gathering witness statements from fishermen. The corpse had been wearing nothing save a pair of trousers and carried nothing to identify him. The head had been badly beaten, one of its eyes was missing and for some bizarre reason, the tongue had been torn out.

"There is certainly evidence of pulmonary oedema," Max intoned, as if addressing a bunch of first year medical students in a broad Edinburgh accent. "And there is water in the lungs, as you might expect. But drowning wasn't the main cause of death."

"Then what did he die of ?" asked Grayling.

"Phenobarbital – or possibly amobarbital. I'll be a hundred per cent certain when I've had a chance to conduct more tests."

"So he was drugged ?"

"Yes, and then pushed into the water, I would imagine. The barbiturate would have suppressed his breathing. Even if he hadn't been pushed into the sea, he would have had enough of the stuff in his bloodstream to cause death from asphyxia."

"What about the tongue ?"

"What about it ?"

"Was the tongue cut out before or after death ?"

"Before death, as it happens, though I would hope it was when the victim was unconscious. Now why would somebody do that ?"

"Why indeed ?"

"There's also something quite interesting here you might wish to examine," Cameron continued, pointing to the deceased's abdomen. Grayling looked at the naked corpse before him. He was staring at the body of a middle aged man. In his youth he might have been good looking, he thought. He had a well proportioned face,

A Cromer Corpse

the teeth were well preserved and on the middle finger of the right hand was an ornate gold ring with a large diamond inset. He was fair haired, almost Italian looking. Cameron stood back to give his colleague a closer look. Grayling was staring at a small pentagram. It had been carved into the flesh of the abdomen just above the testicles.

"Done with a sharp knife – probably a thin kitchen knife, one with a pointed end. Diameter probably about an inch I should say," Cameron observed.

"The pubic hair…"

"Yes, I know. Shaved off. Whether the victim did that to himself we can't know. Least not at present. Of course some people do it for kicks."

"But why a pentagram ?"

"Don't know. Adds a certain mystique, though, doesn't it ?" Cameron grinned. Grayling stared back at the broad, coarse face and shock of unruly ginger hair. At times there was something positively repulsive about Cameron.

"There's little else I can tell you," Cameron went on. "He was in good health. Quite fit for his age. Contracted gonorrhea in the past. Was a smoker and probably drank too much. The liver was a little enlarged. Enjoyed a large meal comprising a beef casserole and vegetables approximately two hours before death. It's possible his food was laced with the barbiturate. There was nothing on the body to identify him, you said ?"

Grayling nodded.

"Well, nil desperandum. Dental records may give us a lead. He's had quite a few bridges done and there are some gold fillings. Obviously went to a good dentist."

"Is that all ?"

"There is something else. See here on the ankle ?"

"The red mark ?"

"Yes. Looks as if he was bound by the leg to something – a structure under water, perhaps. Oh, and

A Cromer Corpse

another thing: his trousers were full of coins. We can only assume they were placed there to weigh the body down. Maybe whoever did this didn't know how to tie a reef knot. Anyway, that's it."

Grayling thanked Cameron, left the morgue, then made his way to the sea front. Although it was only early morning, the air was hot, the streets busy with the hustle and bustle of tourists. He needed some fresh air before going back to Norwich. Outside the Falcon pub he paused for a moment and leaned over the railings, staring out past Cromer pier at the broad, flat horizon of the sea. The body had been picked up about a mile up the coast from here. Knowing the tides and the approximate time of death, he figured the victim had been dropped into the sea somewhere near Morton or Wells. The chances were the murderer was a local man. But whoever had done this had acted out of premeditation. This was surely no crime of passion or the result of a drunken brawl. Morton and Wells were relatively small communities. He would check with missing persons when he got back to HQ and see if it yielded results.

He fumbled in his jacket pocket for a packet of cigarettes and in doing so unearthed the letter he had been sent yesterday. Lighting a cigarette, he then unfolded it and re-read its contents:

"Dear Charles, Thought I'd drop you a line to let you know I'll be coming up to Morton to live on a permanent basis. I don't know if you remember me but if I mention the name of my old pal Glenister of the Met, it may ring bells. I hope so. Happy hours spent together on the Countryman project in the bad old '70's. Anyway, if you still do remember me, and if you fancy a drink for old time's sake, I am your old buddy John

A Cromer Corpse

(Bottrell). PS: Here's my mobile number, though you can find me at Hautbois Lodge from July 26th onwards."

Grayling smiled to himself and placed the envelope back in his pocket. Of course he remembered John Bottrell. How could he forget him ? The bright boy of the squad with his pretty wife Frances. The last thing he heard Bottrell had had some sort of breakdown and left the Force. He must ring and arrange a meet. He finished his cigarette, smelt the salt air once more, then turned and made his way back to the car.

A Cromer Corpse

CHAPTER TWO

The Masonic lodge was a tall, imposing building situated in a wide street in Saxborough Village. With its ionic pillars and mock Elizabethan chimneys, it stood like a sentinel at the top of a hill, overlooking the pier and harbour. On a fine day the Morton Spit could be glimpsed from the windows of the upper storey, but today, a day of thick sea mist, was not one of those fortuitous days.

Today was special, for it marked the Ritual of the Initiation to the First Degree. In a room outside the Lodge room the Tyler, Alex Smith and the candidate were busying themselves in readiness to meet the Worshipful Master. Already the young man in question had removed his outer clothing and was starting to unbutton his shirt in readiness for the elaborate ritual which was to follow. As the candidate rolled up his left trouser leg, the Tyler glanced nervously at the ornate clock above them. It was already ten o'clock and still there was no sign of The Master. Where on earth could he be ?

Alex Smith had conducted numerous initiation ceremonies like this one but never before had The Master been so late. The other Brethren looked nervously at their watches. This was most irregular, thought Smith. Montague Druitt was a man of predictable habits and punctuality. A Master Mason, Druitt had been Master of the Lodge for many years. An authority of the history of Freemasonry, he had a charismatic and sometimes authoritarian manner which

A Cromer Corpse

impressed Smith. From an early age, Smith had been fascinated with occult societies and before gravitating to Freemasonry, had dabbled both in Druidry and Wicca. The fact that Druitt had once been widely known in Somerset as a Wiccan high priest merely added to his kudos in Smith's opinion. No wonder, then, that he revered The Master. Besides which, Druitt was striking in appearance. A tall, blonde haired figure with a classical build, his penetrating blue eyes had an almost hypnotic quality. Some people just emanated power and Druitt had that power. When he entered the Lodge, you felt it. Like an electrical current, it brought you up with a start. And when Druitt spoke, you listened. That soft, Irish lilt had a gravity and authority you just couldn't ignore.

If Druitt didn't arrive soon, Smith reflected, the ritual would have to be conducted by the immediate Past Master, his partner Bradley Evans. Although that would not present a problem, it was far from satisfactory. The inauguration of a new Brother was an important event and required Druitt's presence.

"Excuse me a moment," Smith whispered to Evans. "I must make a phone call."

Evans nodded knowingly and made his way to the lobby. But when Smith rang Druitt's mobile there was no reply. He snapped the phone shut and made his way back to the Lodge room.

"No answer I'm afraid," he said. "We'll just have to get on with it."

* * *

Some time in the night Bottrell woke. For several moments he sat bolt upright in bed, staring into the

A Cromer Corpse

darkness until at last he could make out the edges of the furniture, the shape of the window and the faint glow of the moon on the sea beyond. He stretched out his hand and felt Melanie's back. Her warmth and stillness gave him reassurance.

Slowly, he got out of bed, trying not to waken her, moved over to the window and drew back the curtain fully. A half moon, partly obscured by cloud and mist, hung above the bay, casting an eerie glow on the pier. Far out to sea he could pick out the lights of an oil tanker. The broad, flat sweep of the coastline, with its humped dunes, was so utterly unlike the ragged cliffs of Cornwall to which he had become accustomed.

Fragments of the dream slowly came back to him. He was in a boat, what sort of boat he could not be sure of, but he was lying on his back, staring up at the black night sky. For some reason he couldn't speak or move his arms or legs. Although he was dreaming it was as if he were wide awake. He could hear a voice some way off, a man's or a woman's he couldn't be sure which. His head ached, his eyes pained him. He wanted to sleep, yet something inside him told him he had to keep awake. He knew that inside his jacket pocket was a phone. If only he could reach it with his hand. But his hand was a dead weight attached to the end of his arm. Then the night sky was blotted out momentarily and he saw a shape hovering over him. He was losing focus now, couldn't make out the words... The voice was strangely familiar. That someone was pulling at his leg, lifting it. Something rough and hard was chafing his skin.

Confused memories began racing through his mind. He remembered the meal, then leaving some place, where was it ? Returning to his car. It was dark, he

A Cromer Corpse

recalled now. He'd bent over to put his key in the car door. Then there was an arm round his neck, he was struggling, there was a sharp blow to his head, then blackness.

He forced his eyes open. The night sky again, the smell of the salt sea, sound of water lapping against the boat. Once more he tried to speak but it was useless. His eyes closed and he lost consciousness.

The memory of the dream had faded now. Beyond the window a low sea mist had begun to drift across the water, giving it a strange translucence. Suddenly it felt cold standing here. He moved from the window and made his way back to bed. For a long while he lay on his back, conscious of the slight movements of the sleeping Melanie, knowing that she too must be dreaming. From far off, out at sea, came the boom of a passing ship's horn. Its low, melancholy sound seemed to him profoundly sad. An image of Frances' face passed before him, then dissolved. He closed his eyes, trying to shut out the memories of her and reached out to touch Melanie. Comforted, he began to drift back into sleep. When finally he awoke it was daylight.

* * *

Bottrell peered at the alabaster tablet in Morton church. The inscription read:

"Though gifts of Nature yet thy Gifts of Grace
The all devouring grave cannot Deface.
Witness thy Godly Life, thy blessed End,
Thy Conflicts and they Conquest of ye Fiend,
When to thy Present Friends Thy Dying Breath

A Cromer Corpse
Did sounde thy joyful triumph over Death.
Thy sacred ashes in the earth shall rest
Till Union make both soule and Body Blest."

    Carved into the frame were a skull, an hour glass, the grave digger's tools, a coffin and a reversed torch, all grim reminders of our shared mortality. His reverie was broken by Melanie who touched him on the forearm.
    "Bad thoughts ?" she quizzed. He shrugged.
    "I'm okay," he said. "Quite a remarkable church, isn't it ?"
    Melanie gazed round at the ornate thirteenth century nave and the font with its four saints.
    "And quite a remarkable village too," she said. "There used to be a church here in Saxon times but it was destroyed by marauding Vikings – about the same time Saxborough Priory was destroyed."
    They were now standing in the porch. From here they could see the town, stretching out below them and to their left the broad sweep of the Morton estate. "Over there is Hautbois Hall," Melanie continued, "once the manor house."
    "Who lives there ? Squire of the Manor ?"
    "No, a gay couple, Bradley and Alex. They run the antique dealers in town. Been there for about ten years. Before that the Hall was a psychiatric clinic. And before that it used to belong to Monty Druitt. I mentioned him on the phone to you."
    "I remember."
    "He lives in the Watch House close by the Spit with his partner Helen."
    "Your boss."
    "Yes, my boss."

    Monty Druitt, thought Bottrell. Somehow the name rang a bell, but he couldn't recall where from.
    "And look. That's us, over at the Lodge !"

A Cromer Corpse

She was pointing to a small speck of a building between the sea and the Hall.

They made their way down winding streets, past the clock tower, the Masonic Lodge and the remains of Saxborough Priory, until at last they reached a long line of Georgian houses set well back from the road. In the centre of the terrace was a bow-fronted building bearing the sign "Ariel Books."

"See you at lunch time ?" Melanie asked him. Bottrell nodded.

"One o'clock. The Running Hare."

She knocked on the door of the bookshop and a tall, red-haired woman in her early fifties appeared in the doorway, smiling.

Before taking his leave and making his way down to the harbour Bottrell peered in through the window. There was a wide variety of second hand books on arcane and occult subjects, ranging from Montague Summers' "The Geography of Witchcraft" to a work on medieval grimoires. Melanie's part time job at the bookshop had certainly been good for her, he reflected. Although she had been here for a comparatively short time, she had already made herself known in the community. Maybe the new start and the passage of time would begin to mend her wounds.

He passed on, down Quay Street and the ruins of Saxborough Priory towards the pier. As he grew closer he could see two police cars parked by the harbour wall. He peered over. On the foreshore a collection of uniformed policemen were conducting a fingertip search of the beach. His curiosity aroused, he was about to duck under the barrier tape which barred his entry to the steps when he heard a familiar voice booming at him.

"Sorry sir. No admittance. This is a crime scene."

A Cromer Corpse

He spun round and there stood Charles Grayling. The face was older, greatly lined, the hair was white as snow now, yet there was no mistaking the hawk nose and penetrating blue eyes of his old sparring partner.

"John, as I live or die ! My God you've aged !"

He stretched out a hand like a flipper, shaking Bottrell's hand vigorously.

"The same could be said for you !" Bottrell replied, grinning. You got my letter ?"

Grayling nodded.

"I was going to give you ring. But now it seems I don't need to."

"So what gives ?" Bottrell enquired pointing to the slow patrol of policemen inching their way along the beach.

"Murder. Victim was caught in a fishing net by one of the small vessels working off Cromer. According to tidal currents, I guess he may have been dumped in the sea around here. A bit of a wild guess on my part, but then, why not ?"

"Any idea who the murdered man is ?"

"Not at present. There was nothing on him. Also the head was badly mutilated, the tongue was torn out and someone had cut a pentagram into his groin."

Bottrell raised an eyebrow.

"Some kind of ritual murder maybe ?"

"Who knows ? From what Glenister tells me, that's rather more your department. How is the old bugger by the way ?"

Bottrell smiled. "His usual cantankerous self when last I saw him. That was a while back when I was living in Cornwall."

Bottrell told Grayling about the St Sampson murders and of his narrow escape from death. His old colleague lit a cigarette and looked thoughtful. "And how are you now ?" he asked quietly.

A Cromer Corpse

"Recovered – well, mostly recovered, though I still have some trouble with my left lung."

Grayling smiled. "I did a spell of duty in Cornwall many years ago. Didn't know that, did you ? I was a young DC at the time. I remember my first case vividly. Involved a farming family down on the Lizard. The wife and two daughters had disappeared. Supposed to have gone to Scotland to stay with relatives. Turned out the husband had buried them in quick lime in a field at the back of the farm house. I shall never forget the place. You remember that film with Dustin Hoffman – "Straw Dogs" ?"

Bottrell nodded.

"It had that same claustrophobic atmosphere. The village, I mean. Of course that was way back in the '60's. Way before your time. I guess things have changed since then. It's all pixies and pasties these days."

Bottrell laughed. "And second home owners of course. Just like Norfolk," he ventured, taking his pipe out of his jacket pocket and filling it.

"So why the move to Norfolk then ?"

"My partner – Melanie – she sold up and moved here. Her mother's in a nursing home in Cromer."

"You're not working then ?"

"Did some freelance work for a private detective agency in Truro some months back, but no, nothing since then."

"So you'll be sticking around for a while ?"

Bottrell scribbled his land line number on a scrap of paper and gave it to Grayling. "Give me a ring. When you're not working that is."

Just then there was a shout from below. They both peered over the railings and saw an officer pointing to something in the waves. Another officer had a stick and

A Cromer Corpse was pulling at a sodden bundle of clothes on the foreshore.

"Looks like we just got lucky," said Grayling.

*   *   *

Mrs Edith Gavell had just arrived at her holiday cottage that morning. One of a short row of fishermen's cottages set back from the Morton dunes, she had booked it earlier in the year because of the area's reputation for wading birds. It was a fine summer's day, the sea mist had finally dispersed and she had decided to set out early, armed with a stout stick and her old army rucksack.

It was when she reached the long flat beaches which curved out into the North Sea that she noticed the car. It lay at the end of a track and was practically concealed by a collection of tall beech trees. Whoever had left it here had clearly done so in a hurry, for one of the wheels was stuck in a ditch. Perhaps the car has been abandoned while the owner seeks assistance, she thought, as she approached the car. She peered in at its contents. Several papers were strewn onto the back seat and there was a book entitled "Medieval Pagan Mythology" lying on the floor. She was about to withdraw when she heard a ringing. She looked in again. There, on the floor of the passenger side was a mobile phone. Involuntarily, she pulled at the door and, to her surprise, it opened. Careless, she thought, picking up the phone.

"Hello ?" she said.

"Monty ?" asked the voice at the other end. I'd like to speak to Monty Druitt. Look, who is this ?"

It was only when she put the phone down she noticed the bloodstains on the dashboard and steering wheel. It

A Cromer Corpse
looked like they had been there for a while and there was quite a bit of blood, so much of it, that she began to feel sick.

A Cromer Corpse

CHAPTER THREE

And when she woke the following morning, the bandages swathing her face, she began to remember. She recalled the house, a Tudor manor house, set in its own grounds, concealed from the road by tall oak trees. She remembered the tall chimneys and the elaborate leaded windows and above all the peacocks, their mournful cries filling the soft summer air.

Her mother dressed in white, a long cotton dress it was and around her neck the amber necklace her father had given her on her thirtieth birthday. And her long, blonde hair, flowing over her brown shoulders and her father's rugged face, the blue eyes sharp but kind.

And when she raised her hand to her poor damaged face, she recalled all this and much more besides. Recalled the tall man who greeted them on that late summer afternoon, and the insects buzzing around his head as he opened the door and stood smiling at them in the cool brown oak interior. And when her mother stretched out her hand to greet this man in his red kaftan she knew at once that this was more than mere friendship for she caught the look in her father's face, a look of anguish mingled with despair and she wished then that they had not come to this place, as she had wished so many times since then. But he hugged her father and they went inside and the hallway and the high - ceilinged rooms smelled of incense and there was laughter coming from the upstairs somewhere and the dull, insistent thump of rock music.

A Cromer Corpse

She lay back in bed as the nurse spoke softly to her. How vivid it all seemed now. Though it was years ago, she recalled it all as if it were only yesterday, the high, carved plaster ceilings, the rooms with their African statues, the young men and women, their hair in braids, smoking dope. And all the while he was there, moving among them like some guru, replenishing their glasses, talking to each of them about The Great Ritual. And in her innocence she wondered what that was. Later, as she lay awake in bed, in the small room at the back of the house, and heard the chanting and the insistent beat of the African djembes and crept along the landing and peered down between the banisters, she began to understand what that phrase meant. For there, in a circle, stood the visitors, all of them naked except for her mother and the tall man with the sharp eyes which looked right through you. And as the drum beats grew faster, they twisted and turned this way and that, their voices ululating until at last they reached an exultant pitch. But she could not comprehend the words. Feeling fear, she drew back from the banisters, seeking the security of her room.

The pain was flooding into her left cheek now as she recalled something else. The ride into the night, the tall blonde man at the wheel of the estate, her mother seated alongside him, she and her father in the back, the sound of heavy rock filling the car, the dank smell of the countryside in her nostrils as the driver drove too fast down narrow country lanes. "We're going too fast," she'd said but her voice was lost amid the noise and the chatter of her mother and the driver as they passed dark woods and made their way down into a deep valley.

The warning came too late for in a second the driver had swerved to avoid an oncoming car and they were hurtling over the edge and into the swollen waters of the

A Cromer Corpse

river. She remembered little else of that night save for the screaming, the pain and the weight of her father's lifeless body pressing down on her. But all that was long ago she told herself as she rang the bell and the nurse came to give her the painkillers. It was another time and another place but still the pain and the sense of loss came flooding back to her and it seemed as if it were only yesterday.

* * *

"It was really quite exciting in a morbid sort of way," Edith confessed to her friend Ethel. They were sitting in the Priory Tea Rooms, just off Abbey Street. Ethel, a frail spinster like her companion, had just poured the tea and was listening avidly to her friend's account. An admirer of Miss Marple, she had only once encountered real-life crime, when her handbag had been stolen in the Fulham Road. But that was when she had been much younger.

"What was morbid about it ?" Ethel persisted.

"Oh I didn't tell you, did I ? There was blood, you see, a good deal of it. It was all over the steering wheel and dashboard. And then the phone rang. Well, no, that was before I'd noticed the blood. Anyway, I picked it up. I don't know why. I just picked it up and answered it. There was this man on the other end. He was asking for someone called Monty. Of course I had to explain why I was answering the phone and why I wasn't Monty. It was a bit embarrassing. I suppose I could have been arrested for burglary or something, I told him who I was and he kept asking me questions like where was the car, you know, all sorts of things."

"And then ? And then what happened ?"

A Cromer Corpse

Ethel had become aware that a silence had descended on the tea rooms and faces were turned in their direction.

"Then he told me to stay put and said I should phone the police."

"And you did ?"

"Why, of course I did, Ethel."

* * *

By the time the small crabber moved out into the bay it was already growing dusk. Peter Riscorla stood on the deck, scanning the horizon through a pair of stout Russian binoculars. He was searching for the small Dutch fishing vessel, the subject of his weekly rendezvous. Riscorla, a tall, swarthy man in his mid forties, was unusually tense this morning. Three times he had phoned the Dutchman and three times he had got voicemail. He was particularly concerned since the operation closely involved Druitt. It was Druitt who had forged the initial links with the Dutchman, Druitt who had gone to Amsterdam made the arrangements and Druitt who acted as overseer. Riscorla, who ran the risk, took a hefty percentage of the profits. It was a two man operation and that was the beauty of it. Fewer crew, fewer mouths to blab. Parker, his fellow fisherman, he had known all his life.

For twenty years they had sailed together and they knew every twist and turn of the Norfolk coastline. Neither was this their first taste of contraband. Ten years ago it had been tobacco but now the stakes were higher. Each of the white, one kilo bags was worth its weight in gold. Over the last five years Riscorla had amassed a small fortune, although outwardly maintaining an impoverished image. He played much on his immigrant

A Cromer Corpse

origins. A son of a Portugese fisherman who had settled here in the early 60's, fishing had been his life, but the skills he had learned on those long voyages with his father had provided him with a great advantage for his present endeavour.

Suddenly Parker pointed to a speck on the horizon. "Look ! Over there !" Riscorla adjusted his binoculars. There it was, the small black and white trawler, heading straight towards them, the ebbing sun glinting on its port side, a great mass of cloud behind it. He shut the engine down and anchored, the deep reverberation fading. Then there was silence save for the melancholy cries of gulls, wheeling their way in circle around the vessel.

The sky was fading fast now and the inky black clouds from the east filled the horizon line so that the single light from the Dutch trawler looked like a searchlight in the gathering gloom. The two men stood in silence on the deck, Parker lighting one of his gauloises and coughing periodically. Riscorla was unusually tense, he thought, all the while scanning the calm sea with his binoculars. He was usually more relaxed than this. It was a voyage the two men were used to. What could be troubling him ?

* * *

"What do you make of it ?" asked Grayling.

The SOCO team, who had arrived around mid-afternoon, were standing in a circle round the abandoned vehicle, save for one white-suited figure who was down on his hands and knees, testing the back of the car seat for bloodstains. The tallest of the four, pushed back his

A Cromer Corpse

hood. Lean-faced and dark-haired, there was something of the predator about him. "A reasonable amount of detail as it happens."

He leaned over and pointed through the driver's side. "There are low velocity spatters on the steering wheel, fairly large ones here and there."

"Meaning ?"

"Meaning he was attacked at close range from the passenger side with a sharp object. My guess is he was hit more than once, though."

"How do you figure that out?"

"Because he tried to get out through the driver's door before he was hit a second time. You see these elongated stains with spines or projections of blood?" Grayling looked.

"That's how we know. And if you look here on the floor beneath the passenger seat you'll see these rounded bloodstains. That means whoever hit him sat holding the weapon for a while before getting out of the car. We also found signs of disturbance on the ground alongside the vehicle." He was now pointing to a series of impressions in the earth by the driver's side.

"Looks as if the body was dragged along the ground here," Grayling observed.

"That's right. We've found impressions of two sets of footprints here – both trainers, one set with minimal wear, the other with extensive wear. The minimal wear set are a size five, the other much bigger – a ten."

"So the attacker had an accomplice then ?"

"Possibly. Or maybe there was a child present."

"How do we know they weren't prints from the old woman who discovered the car?"

"That's possible, though we did pick up a small sized print with the luminol from beneath the back seat."

"Well get that checked. Thanks. Anything else?"

A Cromer Corpse

"There are a number of fibres in the car. Take us a while to sort that out."

Grayling was about to ask a further question when he was interrupted by the strident voice of Max Cameron, who was now standing behind Grayling and the SOCO, listening in to the tail end of their conversation.

"Anything useful?" he asked.

Grayling briefed him. "We found a passport in the glove compartment," he added. Cameron opened the passport and looked at a photo of a good looking, fair haired man in his middle years.

"A good match," he said, "though the blood will provide confirmation. So what happened here?"

"Blunt force weapon, struck twice on the right side. Then he was dragged from the car, probably by two people."

"Dragged where ?"

"We don't yet know. The lads are searching the bushes for evidence."

"And the murder weapon ?" Cameron asked, hopefully.

"Not yet. Try me in six hours maybe."

"If only I had the time, laddie. Who is this Monty Druitt, anyway ?"

"Local man, lived at the Watch House in Morton with his partner. They ran an occult bookshop there. Apparently he was something of a character."

"And the wife ?"

"Partner," Grayling corrected him.

"The partner hadn't noticed him missing ?"

"He'd told her he was taking a flight to Amsterdam from Norwich airport. She said she'd phoned his mobile a couple of times but he hadn't got back to her. He had a business associate there. That was three days ago. He'd been due back yesterday morning but when he didn't show up she'd guessed he'd been delayed in

A Cromer Corpse

Amsterdam. There were also several messages on his phone we found in the car from an Alex Smith – local freemason. Druitt had been due to attend one of their Lodge meetings in Morton yesterday but he never showed."

"You interviewed the partner yet ?"

Grayling shook his head.

"Early days yet, Max. I want this lot sorted first. You'll give me that result on the blood traces before I wheel her in ?"

"You'll have the results by lunchtime. Oh, and if you find the murder weapon, it would be a great help."

A Cromer Corpse

CHAPTER FOUR

She soon became familiar with the Tudor mansion. Her parents would visit at least four times a year, sometimes more, to conduct their rituals with the man who became known to her as "uncle." Of course, he wasn't her real uncle, but that was the epithet her father had given him. It was not until she was eight years old that she came to know his real name and by that time the damage had already been done.

On the four occasions of the year her parents would perform what they called "Sabbats." These were elaborate rituals to coincide with the seasons of the year. A great number of people attended these rituals. They came from far and wide from across the West Country, some from as far away as West Cornwall. Some were conventionally dressed when they arrived, others adopted the costume of the hippy. There must have been two to three hundred of them in all. The mansion could well accommodate them. Its labyrinthine rooms and corridors seemed to swallow them up.

On the top floor "uncle" had his own suite of rooms and it was here, one summer afternoon, that he invited her into his study. She could remember the occasion still to this day: a long, book-lined room, the walls hung with oil paintings, many of them frightening to her impressionable mind. She recalled one in particular: it was of a goat figure with cloven feet. He was seated on top of a hill. Behind him was a grove of trees. He was surrounded by strange, misshapen, satyr figures who appeared to be participating in a dance. She couldn't

A Cromer Corpse

recall much more of the painting save for one detail which long afterwards continued to disturb her. They had red, slatted eyes, eyes that burned with malevolent intent.

As soon as "uncle" invited her into the room, he had given her a small teddy bear. Then he had talked for a long while. He had spoken of the faery folk, those little beings who were invisible to grown ups. Had she ever seen faeries ? She admitted that once she had, though it was some while ago and she had never told her parents about the incident. "Then let it be our little secret," uncle had said.

From that moment she had trusted uncle, had grown to love his big face and the eyes that seemed to explore every inch of her soul. She knew then that uncle could be relied upon. She could tell him things that her parents never needed to know and he would always listen, listen with an intentness which she grew to admire. And each time she knocked on the door of his study he would let her in and he would always have some gift for her: a tiny crystal, a small toy. Once he had given her an exquisite ivory unicorn. "Uncle is so kind to children," her mother had said, smiling. "He is so kind to everyone."

* * *

After leaving Grayling by the pier, Bottrell decided he would take a walk southwards and explore some of the landscape around the Morton estate. Part of his route ran along what was known as the "Peddar's Way". Once a massive military road running from Suffolk to Holme on the Norfolk coast, the path afforded glimpses of the sea, then curved back on itself to bisect the estate.

A Cromer Corpse

He'd read a number of theories as to the origin of the route, one being that a Roman ferry once linked Holme to the Lincolnshire coast on the other side of the Wash. His own theory was that it had been built to dominate the indigenous Celtic tribe known as the Iceni after their revolt against rule, when they were led by the legendary Boudica.

Whatever the truth was, it was a fine day for a stroll. He made his way past a small row of fishermen's cottages, gradually climbing until he reached the top of a high cliff. From here he could see the broad sweep of the bay, and to the south, scattered coastal villages, each with their distinctive square church towers, gleaming in the morning sunlight.

He moved on, past The Watch House, then made his way amid dunes onto the narrow stretch of land known as The Spit. Disturbing oyster catchers and terns as he walked, he was soon able to command a view of the Morton estate. On either side of him was nothing but blue sea and the mingled sounds of sea birds as they wheeled above him in the azure sky.

Far off, in the distance, just below Morton Wood, he could make out the iron age barrows which Melanie had told him about. Legend had it that that this was one of the burial grounds of the Iceni and that in the largest of the five barrows lay the remains of the warrior queen herself. He took out his binoculars and trained them on the barrows. He could see a group of a dozen people moving about there. It was clearly an excavation. He walked back along the edge of the Spit, past Hautbois Lodge and The Mere and took the small footpath from the Peddar's Way which led up the hill. When he got to the top, a young woman in a yellow jacket hailed him.

A Cromer Corpse

"What are you doing ?" he asked.

"School of Archaeology. UEA," she replied. "We're excavating the barrows."

"Found anything yet ?"

"Quite a lot. A good supply of pot shards. Plus a small gold torc, quite a find !"

"No warrior queen yet, though ?"

She smiled.

"Not so far. We'll let everyone know when that happens."

He smiled at her and moved on, past the imposing façade of Hautbois Hall, then, glancing at his watch and realising it was lunchtime, double-backed towards the town and his rendezvous with Melanie in The Priory Tea Rooms.

* * *

Chief Inspector Grayling stared through the grimy first floor window into the street below. Although it was only 9am, the sun had already risen over the roof of Norwich City Hall and the stale fumes from passing rush hour traffic drifted up through the open window. It had been a long and eventful night in Norwich. A stabbing in the Prince of Wales Road, a domestic in Hellesdon and an early morning burglary at the Spar shop on the Earlham Road.

"So what about the car ?" he asked Cameron.

"A lot of detail, old chum."

"But anything significant ?"

"We found several pubic hairs – some blonde, some dark. There were also two head hairs – also blonde. The infrared showed they'd been bleached."

"A woman's, then ?"

A Cromer Corpse

"Most likely."

"And what about the car tracks?"

"Still looking at those. The other car was most probably a small saloon – something like a Clio or Micra. Can't be certain yet. Anyway, it's a car with a small wheelbase. The front tyres were quite worn and had a distinctive number of flat spots, so they'll be relatively easy to match."

"When you find the right car," Grayling interrupted.

He was beginning to sweat. He removed his jacket, placing it on the back of his chair.

"Yes, when we find the car."

"Alright, Max. If anything else comes up, just keep me informed."

"Don't I always?" sighed Cameron.

When Cameron had left, he opened the autopsy file and perused its contents. The bloated body of Montague Druitt stared back at him from the photo. *Blunt force trauma. A round-headed hammer the most likely weapon. Wound one inch in diameter. Additional crush injuries to the skull administered post mortem. Symbol of five pointed star carved into abdomen above the genitals.* He looked up for a moment, fingering the packet of cigarettes in his trouser pocket. So what was it, then? Premeditated or a crime of passion? Maybe the accomplice moved the body some while after the attack. At that point in time the victim must have been still alive, though probably unconscious. And the barbiturate. When had that been administered? Before or after the attack? The footprints suggested one of the attackers might have been a woman. Or a child? Unlikely. And what about the pentagram and the shaved genitals? A search of the national computer had revealed nothing about Druitt. All they knew was Druitt was wealthy, that he was estranged from his wife and that he had an interest in the occult. Oh, and that he was a freemason.

A Cromer Corpse

The latter probably didn't amount to much. After all, Grayling was a freemason, as were many of his colleagues in the Force. As for his partner, Margaret Jones, she was an unlikely suspect. Besides, she wasn't a blonde. Then there was the wife... He sighed. It looked like this wasn't going to be one of those cut and dried cases.

* * *

Helen Druitt pulled the hairbrush through her long blonde hair, then, placing it on the dressing table, stared at the face in the mirror. She had just turned fifty two and already deep frown lines etched her face. She had once been told that she had the face of a model with high cheek bones and deep set eyes. But that had been many years ago when she and Monty were living at the Big House in an age when men paid compliments to attractive women without fear of censure.

She still remembered the occasion only too well. The man who had said those words was one of Monty's many acquaintances. A photographer by profession, he had insisted on taking her photo in one of the upper rooms of The Grange. He had been genteel and sensitive in his dealings with her. Over drinks she had posed for him, while beneath them, in a number of rooms, the party raged and drugs were passed freely among Monty's associates and fellow Wiccans.

Helen went along with the "happenings", as Monty described them. Secretly, she enjoyed meeting the bohemian fringe of society which Monty seemed to attract, but she was never devout in her pagan practices, preferring to keep a part of herself aloof. Monty revelled

A Cromer Corpse

in excess of all kinds but Helen liked to keep apart from the crowd, even at these orgiastic gatherings. Michael. That had been his name. He'd had a kind face and long, sensitive fingers. Who knows ? If she'd allowed things to develop with the benign photographer her life would have worked out very differently.

She still had the photo. It took pride of place on her dressing table now, replacing the photo of Monty and her which she had torn up in a fit of rage a year ago when he had at last admitted to his obsession with Margaret Jones.

Margaret Jones... How she detested the name. A mousy, small-minded, scheming drab, a devious, greedy, unscrupulous whore who had inveigled her way into Monty's affections. And now that Monty was dead she would no doubt play the part of the grieving partner. She was a consummate actress, no doubt about it. She would turn in a polished performance. But beneath that manicured exterior was a woman with a heart of ice. Margaret was a cold, ruthless manipulator and Monty had been a fool not to see her for what she was.

Monty was dead. She had seen his lifeless body, laid out on the mortuary slab only the previous morning. Just a lifeless corpse now, in a room full of lifeless cadavers, the face red and bloated as if it had been battered by rocks. Once it had been a fine face, a classical English face someone had once called it, but now Death's hand had reduced it to nothing more than a piece of livid flesh. It was not Monty as she remembered him: the quick, penetrating eyes, the sharp repartee, that look which could so easily, and so often did, seduce a woman. And the smooth, cultured voice that went with it. All that gone forever, replaced by the stench of corruption and the faint whiff of formaldehyde.

A Cromer Corpse

The young WPC had been solicitous, kind even, but as she had left, an older man in a dark suit had introduced himself to her, said he'd had some questions for her. Just routine. How often she'd heard that in films. What was the other phrase ? "Eliminating people from our enquiries." She'd recalled the letters she'd written to Monty after their separation. When she got home she took them from the drawer of the bedside cabinet and burned every one of them. How long had he been dead, she'd asked ? Five days. She tried to recall what she'd been doing five days ago but when she'd checked her diary she found what she'd been looking for. She'd visited the nursing home with Steven, Monty's brother. They'd gone to see Christine, her mother-in-law. Their object had been to persuade her to change her mind over the redrafting of the will.

All the while she'd been married to Monty, the lands around Hautbois Hall plus the Watch House would have been left to them both on the old woman's death. But Margaret and Monty had persuaded Christine to change her will, making Margaret, not Helen, one of the main beneficiaries. Their visit to Cromer Nursing Home had not been a success. The old woman's mind had been made up. It had been tainted by the insidious urgings of that whore and her consort. James had been livid, storming, red-faced, from the nursing home, cursing the day his brother had set eyes on that "whore of Babylon" as he often referred to her.

Helen stared at her face in the mirror. So maybe that made her a prime suspect, she thought. She must expect the finger of accusation to point at her when the time came. Then so be it. She must be prepared.

A Cromer Corpse

CHAPTER FIVE

By the time he got to The Running Hare Bottrell was already ten minutes late. For an East Anglian pub it had survived the excesses of corporate makeovers rather well. A Tudor building, it still retained its oak beams and original wainscotting. There was no one-armed bandit, the furniture was basic but comfortable and the landlord and his wife friendly. Moreover, the real ale was good.

Perhaps because it was the only pub in Morton, the lunchtime trade was brisk. Bottrell squeezed himself past several office workers to a corner of the saloon bar where he found Melanie sipping the remnants of a red wine.
"Sorry I'm late," he apologised. "Need another ?"

At the bar the talk among the locals was all about the murder. From what Bottrell could glean, as he stood waiting to catch the landlord's eye, Monty Druitt had something of a reputation as an eccentric and as a lady's man. He was about to learn more when his turn came.

Back at the corner table, he started to fish his pipe out of his jacket pocket but when he saw Melanie pulling a face, remembered the ban. PC Britain, he thought.
"Been here long?"
"About twenty minutes. Margaret shut the shop up early. She was too upset to continue. I said I'd cover for the afternoon but she thought it best."
"How is she?"

A Cromer Corpse

"Very distraught of course. She wanted to identify the body but they asked his wife."

"Helen ?"

Melanie nodded.

"There's not much love lost between them. That's partly why she was so upset. But there's also something else." She leaned over to him, conspiratorially. "She told me Monty had had a death threat."

"When was this exactly ?"

"About two weeks ago. Apparently he chose to ignore it."

"What was it? A letter?"

"Yes."

"Did he keep it ?"

"He threw it away. And someone tampered with the brakes of their car."

"Did they report it ?"

"I asked her that. She said they didn't bother. It wasn't the first time it had happened."

She was interrupted at this point by a loud burst of laughter coming from the bar. Bottrell turned to see two men, creased with laughter, facing each other on bar stools. One was bald. He wore a silver ear ring and was flamboyantly dressed in a loud maroon suit with a pink shirt and contrasting yellow tie. The other was smaller, wearing a leather jacket, figure hugging denims and expensive Italian open toed sandals.

"Who's the cabaret ?" asked Bottrell.

"Alex Smith and Bradley Evans. They're the two gay guys I told you about."

"The antique dealers."

"Rumour has it they're loaded. The one on the right had a brief fling with Monty, so rumour has it."

"Recently ?"

"Heavens no. This was when Monty was still living with Helen. Bradley and Monty knew each other before Monty came to Norfolk, when they were both Wiccans."

A Cromer Corpse

"So when did Monty give up being a Wiccan ?"

"I don't exactly know. A while back I suppose. Margaret never said. According to her he preferred to follow his own path. Did you know he was a freemason ?"

"You didn't mention it."

"Sorry. I forget you've only been here five minutes ! You said you bumped into an old colleague of yours?"

"Charles Grayling, yes. I met him by the pier this morning. An old mate from the Met. We worked on Operation Countryman together years back in the '70's. Pornography, corruption – and Freemasonry." He smiled. "Another one ?"

"I'd better not. What was he doing down there ?"

Bottrell glanced back at the bar. Leather jacket leaned over to pink shirt and was placing a reassuring hand on his knee. Pink shirt looked offended. They were no longer laughing. A lover's tiff, Bottrell wondered ?

"They found some articles of clothing on the foreshore. Might have had a connection to the murdered man. Anyhow, I'm seeing Charles tonight. I'll ask him for details. He wants to pick my brains about the affair."

"When this evening ?"

"It's okay. It'll be after dinner – in the pub here."

"Promise me you won't overdo it."

"I promise."

He finished his drink and kissed her. Leather jacket was preparing to leave. His face was like thunder. "Wonder what that was all about ?" he said.

* * *

Helen Druitt lived in a small bungalow some way up the Cromer Road. Small and unpretentious, it was a marked contrast to the Watch House where she and Monty had

A Cromer Corpse

lived for a number of years. She missed the large open fireplace, the cosy, book-lined study and the large garden which she had grown used to over the years.

Leaving Monty had been painful. Theirs had been a long but difficult association. She had never loved a man so much as she had loved Monty but there was a part of Monty's psyche which made him unable to reciprocate that deep passion she felt for him. When Monty loved, he loved only in a physical sense. During those troubled years it was as if he had possessed her, but possession was as far as it went. At the same time there had been others, both men and women. At first she had tolerated his peccadilloes, accepting his promise that it would not happen again. But after the third or fourth infidelity she had despaired of him.

Margaret Jones had been the catalyst. She hated that woman with a passion which knew no bounds and which at times bordered on derangement.

Charles Grayling gazed at the few ornaments in an otherwise bare and soulless lounge. There was nothing here, he pondered, no telling detail which might have given him an insight into this woman. The only real item of interest was a framed photo of Helen Druitt which stood on the sideboard. She was much younger and looked relaxed and happy, unlike the haggard woman who now entered, bearing a tea tray.
"I didn't ask you if you took sugar in your coffee, Inspector?"
"Three please."
"Help yourself to biscuits."
She sat opposite him, her legs crossed tightly under a plain knee length skirt.

A Cromer Corpse

"Just a few questions about your husband, Mrs Druitt," said Grayling, after an awkward silence. "I understand you were separated ?"

"That's right."

"How long ago did you leave him?"

"I didn't leave him. We agreed to part. I wasn't prepared to put up with playing second fiddle."

"You're referring to Margaret Jones, I take it?"

She nodded. "Not only did he insist on having her visit the house, he also started employing her at the bookshop. Now of course she's there permanently. Which is why I left."

There was cold fury in her voice.

"So you don't work for your husband now?"

"It was a partnership. When I left, he paid me back my share in the business. I insisted that he did. I went back to my old job as a librarian at the University."

"Mrs Druitt, can you think of anyone who might have wanted to harm your husband?"

She shrugged her shoulders.

"What does that mean, exactly?"

"Monty knew a lot of people. He had a past."

"In what way?"

"Before he came to East Anglia, mostly. He was a prominent figure in paganism then. He knew a lot of people in the movement."

"This was when you lived in Somerset."

"Yes. And he upset quite a few people when we were there. And some people have very long memories."

"Anybody in particular?"

"I couldn't say. The pagan world is very factional. Do What Thou Wilt And ye Harm None is great in theory but in practice things aren't like that."

"Mrs Druitt, I have to ask you this. Did you hold a grudge against your husband?"

"What do you want me to say? You want me to say I forgave him? You want me to lie? How would you feel

A Cromer Corpse

in my situation? It's not Monty I hated, Inspector. It's that woman. We were relatively happy together before she showed up. I could even forgive him the occasional fling. But her. Conniving. She had it all planned the moment she set eyes on him. The house, the bookshop. She wheedled her way into his affections. And Monty was vain and stupid enough to fall for her. Men aren't at all bright, are they, Inspector?" Her face was red now, her eyes glistening.

"Nonetheless, I must also ask you to account for your movements on July 25th."

"I would have been working that day. At the library."

"And when you finished work ?"

"Finished at 6pm, then came home, made a meal and watched TV for the remainder of the evening."

"Alone?"

"Quite alone."

Grayling sat in the car, compiling his notes, the image of Helen Druitt's tear stained face uppermost in his mind. She had motive. There was no doubting it. That cold, focussed anger was something he had seen before on the faces of vengeful spouses. On the other hand there had been an accomplice. Did Helen have a lover? If she did she was keeping it quiet. He must look into it. And that account of her whereabouts the day Druitt died. She had that off pat. No, she was a cold fish alright. He opened a packet of cigarettes and lit one. Inhaling deeply, he wound down the driver's window and blew the smoke out. From her lounge window, Helen Druitt stared at the car as it drove off down the quiet street. Then she closed the curtains.

* * *

A Cromer Corpse

It was quiz night in The Leaping Hare. Since the pub was packed to full capacity, Grayling and Bottrell were forced to retire to the quaintly entitled "Smoking Room" at the rear of the premises, which was nothing more than a lean to. Grayling was in sombre mood, having spent most of the day at the court in Norwich. He had been giving evidence in an arson case but, despite his best efforts, the defendant had been acquitted. Lighting his briar, Bottrell sat opposite his old colleague, spirals of smoke forming a blue miasma between them. He reflected that although Grayling was older, more lined and had lost most of his hair, his eyes were as keen as ever and his intellect undimmed.

"So you settled in okay?" asked Grayling.

"Fine."

"And Melanie?"

"She's fine. You'll have to have dinner with us. Soon."

"When I can spare the time."

"So how's it going?"

Grayling sipped his malt.

"Early days yet. We have no real leads at present. Interviewed the wife this morning."

"Useful?"

"She's a cold fish. Deeply resentful of her husband, though she pretended she wasn't. Blamed it all on the lover. He had something of a reputation it seemed. Bisexual."

"Yes, when they lived in Somerset. And here. Melanie told me about that. They owned a large property near Wells. Turned it into a sort of hippy commune. But in the end it didn't work out, so they sold up, moved up here and bought the bookshop."

"I gather he was some sort of warlock."

"Yes, he was into modern paganism. A Wiccan. Though I get the impression he'd moved on from that some while back."

A Cromer Corpse

"To what?"

"I'm not quite sure. I'm only basing this on what Mel had gleaned from working in the bookshop."

"According to the wife he had enemies."

"Who ?"

"She wouldn't be specific. I got the impression he'd upset quite a few people in Somerset. Of course she could be making that up. Listen John. You know a deal more about these sorts of matters than I do. Think you can do me a favour and find out about his past associations?"

"I'll do what I can."

Grayling was aware that over the past few years, and especially since the Zennor murder case, Bottrell had amassed a considerable wealth of detail about occult groups in the West Country. The thoroughness of his research never ceased to impress Grayling. During Operation Countryman he had been known jocularly as "The Ferret" because of his single mindedness and persistence.

Bottrell ordered a fresh round of drinks and the two sat silently for a while, listening to the noise from the other bar.

"I wanted to ask your opinion about the mutilations on Druitt's body," Grayling said at last.

"You mean the pentacle?"

"What is the significance of that?"

"Well, obviously it's associated with paganism. It's also known as The Witch's Cross. It forms a continuous protection sign."

"So – what – it's like a crucifix, then?"

"That's its modern use, yes. Though at one time it was sacred to the Earth Goddess Morrigan."

"And who was she?"

"An Irish warrior goddess. A slayer of men."

"That doesn't get us much further, though, does it?"

"Not much, no. Sorry I can't be more helpful."

A Cromer Corpse

The two men finished their drinks, then left the pub and made their way along by the harbour. It was a still, moonlit night. They leaned on the railings, peering down at the waves as they lapped gently at the foreshore below them.

"You get anything from the clothes?" Bottrell asked.

"A small pocket diary. Damaged from the sea water but still largely legible. There are a number of entries. Business appointments, maybe. He made several trips to Amsterdam. We're looking into that. You think this was some sort of ritual murder?"

Bottrell shrugged.

"Perhaps. I'm not sure. But whoever did kill him was surely making a statement."

A Cromer Corpse

CHAPTER SIX

Bottrell stared at the pew ends. Each one carried a small hour glass. For a moment he remained puzzled. Then he'd figured it out. They'd surely been placed here in the 18th Century when sermons were long and tedious. They were a way of measuring the length of the sermon.

A voice interrupted his reverie. He turned to face a tall, dark-haired figure in a cassock. In appearance he was striking, with deep-set eyes, a Roman nose and a pronounced widow's peak, off-setting a high forehead.

"Admiring our bench ends? I'm pleased to meet you. Reverend James Druitt. You're new here, I take it?"
Bottrell introduced himself.
"A friend of Melanie's. She's a personable young woman. And been of great help to Margaret in her recent trouble."
His voice trailed off, as they made their way down the nave together.
"It's quite a close knit community here in Morton, Mr Bottrell, but I'm sure you've already discovered that. That's why this – business – has come as such a blow to many of us. This rood screen is 17th Century you know. It survived Cromwell and is virtually still intact."
Bottrell could feel the tension in this man. He was slightly ahead of him, hunched, hands plunged into his trouser pockets. "It's the story of Cain and Abel," he pointed out. "A story as old as time itself."
"You were on good terms with your brother?" The question was deliberately incisive.

A Cromer Corpse

"I must be honest, Mr Bottrell, and tell you that we were not on the best of terms. There had been a falling out. It was not just the religious difference you see."

"You mean the paganism?"

"Yes, I admit that was difficult for me from the start. Of course, when Monty began all that business we were living separate lives. He was with Helen then, in Somerset, so I saw little of him. Of course, I heard about him from time to time. Helen would send me press cuttings and so on."

"He was well known in the area?"

"Yes, in the local community there. I don't know if you're familiar with the background?"

"I knew he was running some sort of hippy commune near Wells."

"Actually it was a little more than that. He was trying to set up something he referred to as the Gardnerian Foundation."

"What was that exactly?"

"It was intended to be a trust, founded in honour of the late Gerald Gardner."

"The founder of modern witchcraft?"

"Precisely. You've seen our Norman font? Magnificent, isn't it. This little woodwo is the only one of its kind in the whole of East Anglia."

Bottrell quelled his impatience at this digression.

"He got a good deal of financial support from a number of pagan groups in the West Country. But in the end the project fell through."

"Why was that?"

"I'm not entirely sure. There was talk of financial irregularities. Whatever the truth of it was, he succeeded in making quite a few enemies in the pagan community."

"Which is why he left Somerset?"

"And bought Hautbois Hall."

A Cromer Corpse

"I thought that was owned by two antique dealers? What are they called?"

"Alex and Bradley. No, they rent it from Monty. Bradley and Monty have known each other for years. When Monty was short of money, and he wanted to take the lease on the bookshop, he came to an arrangement with them."

"And they're pagans too?"

"Bradley certainly is. I can't speak for Alex. I know it's hardly fashionable to say so, but I don't care much for people of that persuasion." This was said with a faint air of disgust.

"You mean you don't like gays?"

"If you want to put it bluntly, yes."

They had now reached the bell tower. James Druitt looked up.

"They were cast in 1676. And they're still in remarkable condition. As is the Church, despite the Reformation."

"Mr Druitt, can you think of why anyone would wish to kill your brother?"

"I'll be frank with you. Monty was a closed book to me, Mr Bottrell. At least, when he began this journey into the occult. I am of the impression that in recent years he had begun to experiment with a much darker form of magic. As you may be aware, most modern paganism is little more than a harmless form of nature worship. Animism – call it what you like. But Monty had tapped into something altogether different. I came across him working some ritual in Morton Wood, near those old barrows. This was last summer. There was a group of them, all wearing hooded cloaks. And they had a cockerel."

"What? They were performing an animal sacrifice?"

A Cromer Corpse

"Were about to, yes, until I spoilt their fun. That's when I realised Monty had moved on to the voodoo stuff."

"Did you challenge him about it?"

"What difference would it make if I had? He saw me as the enemy. Hardly surprising, really, given my vocation! Whether his partner Margaret was into the dark stuff I couldn't say. I know that Helen wouldn't have stood for it. When I got the news about Monty's death, quite frankly I wasn't surprised. Saddened, yes. After all, those who seek to harm others, well, you know what I mean…"

Bottrell watched the clergyman carefully. They had moved to the porch now and were looking out at the churchyard.

"Do What Thou Wilt But Ye harm None. Isn't that the creed?" he said.

"I believe it is. Now Mr Bottrell, you'll have to excuse me. I have a funeral. Nice to have met you."

Bottrell made his way down the path, glancing back momentarily at the figure of James Druitt. He was examining his watch nervously. All the while he had been talking to Bottrell, the man had seemed on edge. He wondered if there had been a hidden agenda with his brother, something he wasn't prepared to divulge to a stranger. He decided he would contact his old journalist friend Jonathan Goodman of the Western Morning News. If anyone could find out more about Druitt's hippy commune it would be Jonathan. Hadn't Melanie told him the mother was still alive? In a nursing home in Cromer. Maybe he should pay her a visit.

Just then his phone rang.

"Hi John. Its Mel. Where are you?"

A Cromer Corpse

"At the church. Been talking to Monty Druitt's brother."

"D'you mind if Margaret comes round this evening to dinner? I thought it might do her good. Buck her up."

"Fine. See you later."

Closing his phone, he made his way past the pier and the fishermen's cottages towards Hautbois Lodge. A police car flashed past him, siren wailing. He stopped to watch. It was heading in the direction of The Mere. A second car followed, an unmarked vehicle this time. Behind the wheel was Charles Grayling, looking grim-faced. His curiosity aroused, he continued on his journey. But when he got to The Lodge, he carried on up the hill, for in the distance he could already see the blue and white scenes of crime barrier tape, flapping in the wind around the iron age barrows.

* * *

"It's alright. I know him. Let him through."

Grayling was standing by the largest of the barrows. He was in his shirt sleeves, his face was red and bathed in perspiration. Next to him stood the stooped, portly figure of Max Cameron, swathed in the familiar white suit and latex gloves. As Bottrell approached, Grayling turned to greet him.

"Not a pretty sight, I'm afraid. She's been here quite a while."

"Who is she?"

"Don't know yet. Body of a young girl. About ten years old. These guys found her," said Grayling, pointing to a group of onlookers, standing on the other side of the barrier tape. Bottrell recognised one of them as the archaeologist he had spoken to the previous

A Cromer Corpse

morning. "They're from the University," he continued. "Doing a dig here. Apparently these are iron age burial sites which may have some connection with Boadicea. Anyway, when it came to this site, they got rather more than they bargained for. This is Max Cameron, by the way. Max, meet John Bottrell – an old acquaintance of mine from the Met days."

The tall Scot smiled and nodded at Bottrell.

"Pleased to meet you, John."

"I've asked John to have an input into the Druitt case. He has some background in matters relating to the occult."

Cameron looked at Bottrell quizzically.

"Weren't you involved in the Zennor murder case?" he asked.

"That's right."

"I read about that. That must have been quite a shock to you."

Bottrell smiled.

"You could say that."

Grayling looked at his watch.

"I need to get on, gentlemen. Care to take a look John?"

Cameron opened a zip in the SOCO tent and they stepped inside. In a shallow grave lay the remains. Although greatly dessicated, the body was still largely intact. Because it had lain in dry sand, the process of mummification was well advanced. Bottrell stared down at the skull of the cadaver. Although the eyes had gone and the lips were shrivelled and the skin over the cheekbones was a pale yellow, the teeth were clearly those of a minor. The body, which was fully clothed, had been laid out as if in sleep, the long blonde hair splayed around the shoulders, as if someone had taken some care over the arrangement of the deceased.

"Has she been molested?" asked Bottrell.

A Cromer Corpse

"Impossible to say at this stage, given the condition of the body," replied Cameron.

"How did she die?"

"Strangulation by means of a ligature. You see this deep furrow in the tissue of the neck?"

He knelt down to examine the body closer.

"She's been attacked from behind. You can see that from the lateral directions of the marks. It was a thin ligature, possibly a waxed washing line. There are no discernible fibres. And there's something else. Before the ligature was applied, she was struck from behind with a blunt object – struck with considerable force I might add. The top of the cranium has shattered and pieces of the bone have lodged themselves in the brain. The blow would certainly have rendered her unconscious. There's something else of interest – something rather odd. You see how her hands are clasped? When I examined them closely I found fragments of dead flowers held by the fingers. She was holding a posy of wild violets, rosemary and lavender."

"Placed there post mortem?"

"I'm not sure, not judging by the position of the fingers."

Almost as if the girl had been prepared for her own death, Bottrell mused. This was no random killing, then. If she was the victim of a paedophile, why crush her skull before strangling her? The profile didn't fit.

"How long has the body been here?" asked Grayling.

"Not easy to say. You see the mummification? If you look closely, you'll notice there's a gap between the large stones which form part of the tomb. That's allowed the air to circulate round the body and it's kept the sand dry. Perfect conditions for mummification. If you want me to guess, I'd say she's probably been here the best part of a year."

A Cromer Corpse

"We'll check the county's missing persons list for juveniles of course. See what comes up. No sign of a murder weapon?"

"None."

"Oh, one other thing. The archaeologist tells me he discovered the body when he was disinterring a funerary urn – a large pot. What he said was interesting. He told me the pot must have been moved from its original position where the body lay and re-sited above it."

"So why would someone take the trouble to do that?"

"Your guess is as good as mine. I'm just telling you what he told me, Charles."

"Where is he?"

"Over there."

"I'll talk to him."

Bottrell made his way slowly back down the footpath, pausing to look back at the scene on the hill. White coated figures wandered about the improvised tent, their ghostly outlines now partly swathed in mist. It was growing cold. He buttoned his jacket, then reached for his briar and lit it. Up there on the hill he had felt a sudden chill. There was something about the place he didn't care for. The sense of death was overpowering. It wasn't the body of the girl which had so disturbed him. He had seen worse sights than that during his years in the Met. No. There was something else. The hill had an atmosphere. It was a numinous, shifting place, a borderland. Perhaps it had always been a place of the dead, a place where the veil between the living and the dead was at its thinnest. And what of the girl? Why bury her in an iron age barrow? This was not the trademark of a paedophile. It hinted of something darker, more sinister. Her death had been a calculated affair. She had died in a ritualistic manner – almost as if she had been a human sacrifice.

A Cromer Corpse
He finished his pipe, then proceeded down the hill. The sun was lower now and the Mere lay ahead of him, the afternoon sunlight glinting on its calm waters. What dark secrets might it conceal?

A Cromer Corpse

CHAPTER SEVEN

One midsummer's morning she climbed up the hill and sat down on a seat, looking out on the land. A heat haze encircled the surrounding hills. Up here, the claustrophobia which had dogged her all her adult life seemed to diminish. She sat in silence, listening to the rise and fall of a solitary blackbird's song.

She would often come here when she felt troubled. Her "black dog" she called it. That terrible feeling of dark anger and depression which came upon her like an iron cloak, disempowering her, driving her back to that time in her childhood when the troubles had begun. Whatever she did in her adult life, wherever she lived, whoever she tried to love, Black Dog would seek her out, fasten its fangs about her throat, squeeze the life out of her until she felt like a limp rag doll, a bundle of rags and tatters with a burning, overwhelming desire to lash out and harm others who stood in her way.

But of all the days in the year, it was this day, Midsummer's Day, which caused her most grief. For it was on this day, so many years ago now, that she lost her soul and Black Dog came to her for the first time.

She was no more than twelve when it happened. Her parents had driven her down to the Big House. They had arrived late, shortly before the onset of dusk. Already the long drive was littered with visitors, many of them dressed in colourful, piebald outfits, suited for the occasion. All day her mother had been in high spirits, chatting animatedly about the forthcoming ritual to her

A Cromer Corpse

father. They had been here last year of course. But that had been a much less ambitious affair. This year it was special.

On the lawns which faced the Big House they had constructed an enormous figure fashioned from timber and straw. Thirty feet high it stood, a crude, gargantuan figure without a face, the arms outstretched, the legs rigid and doll-like. It was to be the sacrifice, the Midsummer Bonfire.

As the car snaked its way up the long drive, the dark trees gave way to bursts of radiance where small fires had been lit. She caught glimpses of figures, some dancing, some drumming, some semi-naked. She could hear the excitement in their voices, sense the approaching culmination.

Once at the house, "Uncle" greeted them. He smiled at her, stroked her hair. She was clutching the small rag doll he had given her on her previous visit. She smiled back at him. She could trust Uncle, her mother had told her. Uncle was in charge of The Magic.

Then, shortly before midnight the great fire had been lit. Great yellow flames rose into the sky. As the company drummed, the wicker colossus twisted this way and that. The chanting became wild and ecstatic. She and the others, chosen to be the Midsummer Maidens, stepped forwards. Dressed in her long white cotton frock, wearing her floral headband, she threw her garland into the flames. The sweet smells of rosemary, vervain and sage rose into the warm night air. The figure toppled, then crashed to the ground amid whoops and shrieks. There followed an abrupt and eerie silence. Finally, the ritual was over.

A Cromer Corpse

It was the following morning when she found the hut. She had woken early, roused by a blackbird, perched in a bush beneath her window. Rag doll had asked for a walk in the woods before the day grew too hot. She always listened to rag doll, always answered her wishes. She dressed quickly, then slipped downstairs and out into the garden. The house was silent at this hour. Not a soul stirred.

Outside, she smelt the acrid smell of smouldering wood. There were the blackened remains of the wicker woman, lying in a circle of charred earth. She walked on, singing to herself, rag doll swinging at her side, feeling the warm sun on her back. Soon she was into the trees and no longer visible from the house. The great oaks and beeches provided cooling shade and darkness.

The hut lay some way off from the main path. She had seen it once before, on one of their previous forays into the forest, but she had not taken much notice of it then. But today she stopped and stared. She could see the outline of a figure moving about inside. Curious, she hid behind a tall ash tree and watched. After a few minutes the door opened and Uncle emerged, wearing a black robe. He was wiping his hands on a white flannel, and his hands were red. What could he have been doing in there she wondered? Part of her wanted to call out but she held back, she didn't quite know why. It was something about his movements and the way he kept looking round as if he didn't want to be seen. So she waited.

He locked the door to the hut, then made his way back up the path. When he was out of sight, she rolled a log up to the wall of the hut, then stood on it. She could just see in through the grimed window, though her view was partially blocked by a tattered curtain. For several

A Cromer Corpse

minutes she stood there, frozen by fear. Inside, on a long pine table, was the body of a dead crow. The creature was spreadeagled, the beak facing upwards, the yellow eyes staring at her. The wings were outstretched and through the breast of the creature a long steel pin had been thrust.

* * *

He had just got back to the house when the phone rang.
"Goodman here. How's Norfolk, then?"
Bottrell recognised the familiar Geordie voice at once.
"Settling in okay, thanks."
"I hear you have two murders on your doorstep. Sorted them out yet?"
"News does indeed travel fast."
"So it does! You wanted some background on this Montague Druitt character?"
"Go ahead."
"I found out quite a bit actually. He was very active in the Wells area during the mid '70's. Known locally as "The Witch Of The West." Prominent for a while in the Pagan Alliance before he was asked to leave by the organisation. Something to do with irregularities concerning two female members."
"The Pagan Alliance. Remind me."
"It's – or it was – a loose alliance of pagan groups from the West Country. No longer in existence. It covered a wide selection of groups including some of the more whacky forms of paganism."
"So what exactly did Druitt do to get himself pushed out?"
"They won't say. Rumour had it he'd been making a nuisance of himself with these two women."
"What – stalking them?"

A Cromer Corpse

"So it was suggested. Of course we couldn't print that at the time and they wouldn't specify it. But that was the gist."

"Anything else?"

"Yes. He had a large house near Wells. Gravesham Manor. It had been a hotel during the '60's, then fallen on hard times. Druitt turned it into a kind of pagan hippy commune. Used to have large celebrations there. At the peak of his popularity, hundreds used to turn up to the events. Pissed off the locals no end. I've got several archive articles I can send you about it."

"I'd be interested."

"His long term project was to set up a centre for Wiccan studies in honour of his hero, Gerald Gardner."

"The witchcraft guru."

"The same. Anyway, in the end he left."

"Do you know why?"

"Not entirely clear. We reckoned he'd run out of money, run up debts. There was also the business of the child who went missing."

Bottrell removed the pipe from his mouth.

"The what?"

"The missing twelve year old. You didn't know about that?"

"What year was this?"

"1976."

He recalled now. He'd been working on the cold case unit in Bristol at the time.

"What happened?"

"A family had visited one of the celebrations at Gravesham Manor. People used to camp in the grounds – this was a midsummer event. Anyway, a girl went missing. Police made extensive searches and enquiries but she was never found. She just disappeared into thin air. The event brought Druitt a deal of bad publicity. The News of The World brought out a story about Black

A Cromer Corpse

Magic rituals and the like. A year after that Druitt packed up and left."

"And then?"

"I've no idea. He seems to have gone to ground as far as the media were concerned. Anyway, that's the extent of it. I've got quite a bit of stuff here. I can scan it and send it."

"I don't have a PC - or the internet."

"I forget. Rural Norfolk. I'll post it to you.

"Thanks."

"My pleasure. How's the lovely Melanie?"

"Well. She's working for Druitt's partner."

"Maybe there's a story there."

"Just keep your nose out of it."

"I promise to behave."

"You do that."

* * *

The morgue was as Grayling remembered it: cold, stark and cheerless. He was a not infrequent visitor of course, though, since the alterations and renovations had been made last year, those visits had been less frequent. Often these days he liked to deputise the job to one of the other members of his team, for Grayling had an innate aversion to looking at the bodies of the deceased.

Maybe it was to do with his advancing years and the realisation of the finality of death. But whatever it was, on this particular Friday morning in July, he'd wished he were anywhere but here.

Max Cameron pulled back the sheet and they both stared at the remains of the unknown girl.

"Still no idea who she was, then?" he asked.

A Cromer Corpse

"I've got Waverley on it. She's checking through the list. She's narrowed it down to a possible three, one in Suffolk, the other two in the county. Identification's going to be a problem, though."

"Naturally."

"What about the body though? Anything more you can add?"

"More than I was able to tell you six hours ago. No sign of sexual molestation. Cause of death certainly asphyxiation. The stomach contents were interesting. She'd ingested quite a deal of valerian and hemlock before she died."

"And what effect would they have had?"

"The valerian would have induced a narcotic, trance-like state. The hemlock would have killed her."

"Quickly?"

"Quite rapidly. When the blow was delivered to the back of the skull she may well have been semi-conscious, if not unconscious."

"How long ago did she die?"

"Now I've had a chance to check the insect evidence I can tell you fairly exactly. It would have been around late June of last year. That's also backed up by the pollen traces we found on her clothes. Another thing which might prove useful to you. The soil traces we found on her trainers match the soil found here, around Morton."

"Suggesting she was a local girl?"

"That's my guess. Oh, she was also a virgin."

Cameron imparted this information almost as if the fact of her virginity was something exceptional.

"Call me old fashioned, but wouldn't that be normal for a twelve year old girl?"

"Not these days, no. Where have you been during the last decade?"

Grayling ignored the riposte.

"The murder weapon?"

A Cromer Corpse

"That's a difficult one, Charles. I thought at first the wound might have been inflicted with a hammer but these serrations would suggest an axe. But if it *was* an axe it was an extremely blunt one. Not your average axe. You see this scalp wound? It's quite ragged, which means the axe head must have been large, squat in appearance. Almost like one of those stone age flint axes you see in museums."

Max was about to continue his observations when Grayling's mobile rang. It was Waverley.
"Glad I got you sir. I tried earlier but –"
"I was out of range. What is it, Waverley? I'm busy with the pathologist."
"It's about the girl sir."
"What about her?"
"I think we may have struck lucky. Those three you asked me to check from the missing persons database –"
"Get to the point."
"Two of them were no good. Too old for one thing, but the third –"
Grayling sighed. Waverley could be pedantic at times.
"The third girl, Sarah Knowles, went missing last June in the Earlsham area."
Grayling recalled the case now. The teenager had attended a school disco in the town and never returned home. Despite an extensive search she had never been found. There had been a suspicion at the time she had travelled to Scotland to be with her father, but nothing came of that.
"You've spoken to the mother yet?"
"I asked her what her daughter had been wearing when she last saw her. Those designer trainers and the trousers. They seemed to make a match."
"Okay, Waverley. Find out who her GP is. And check the dental records. I'll let Cameron know. And one more thing."

A Cromer Corpse

"Yes sir?"

"Leave the mother to me. Give me her number, will you?"

Grayling made a note of it. He closed the phone and found Cameronl staring at him.

"A break?"

"Seems so."

He looked down at the body.

"No ordinary killing, is it, Max?"

"No indeed. If you want my opinion, Charles –"

"Oh, I certainly do."

"I think we have a ritual killing on our hands."

A Cromer Corpse

CHAPTER EIGHT

Margaret Jones was sitting in the lounge at Hautbois Lodge, sipping a glass of sherry. For the last fifteen minutes Melanie had been busy in the kitchen, putting the finishing touches to the meal, and this had given Bottrell adequate time to examine their guest at close quarters.

She was younger than he had imagined, probably in her early forties he thought, and attractive in an unusual way. Like his former wife, Frances, her face was striking, with prominent dark eyes and soft, pale skin. There was something preraphaelite about her, he thought, as he offered to refill her glass.
"Thanks but I'm fine."

What was it about her that intrigued him? It was not just that she was conventionally good looking. High cheekbones, regular teeth, the straight dark hair cut short to the nape, her clothes carefully matched and chosen, the style colourful, ethnic, a flamboyant red skirt concealing shapely dancer's legs. No, there was something else here, a suggestion of smouldering passion in the dark eyes, some emotion she was holding onto. Despite that, the voice was controlled, the delivery flat, emotionless. She gave nothing away.
"So how are you doing?" he asked as Melanie entered the room, about to announce the meal was ready. There was a pause. Then:
"Feeling a bit better thanks. It came as a great shock to me. Monty and I had been close. Until…" the voice trailed. "…recently."

A Cromer Corpse

"Right," said Bottrell. He glanced at Melanie, expecting a signal.

"Are you okay to talk about it?" asked Melanie, quietly.

"I'm alright, really, Mel. Maybe in a little while. That smells good."

After most of the casserole had been eaten, Margaret finished her wine and sat back in the chair. She looked slightly more relaxed now and there was a colour to her cheeks.

"That detective – Grayling – came to see me yesterday. Asked me questions about Monty."

"How did you get on?" asked Melanie.

"I found it very difficult. We've only been together for a short while. Far shorter than his wife."

"You told him about Helen and the bad feeling she had for the both of you?"

Margaret looked tearful. Her voice was no longer emotionless. Bottrell could sense the strain in it as she spoke.

"I told him about the letters she'd written to me – and to Monty. I kept the ones she sent me but Monty destroyed his. Said she must be barking mad."

"Did you tell him about the brakes on the car?"

"Yes. Of course Monty couldn't prove it was her. I told Grayling we suspected her but that we couldn't prove anything. He said we should have reported it to the police."

"How long ago was this?" asked Bottrell.

"About six months ago now. When the brakes failed Monty crashed the car into a hedge. He was lucky to get away with superficial cuts and bruises and a bit of whiplash. I'm not sure Grayling took it that seriously. He kept asking me questions about Monty's connections with the pagan movement."

"And what did you tell him?" asked Melanie.

A Cromer Corpse

"What could I say? General stuff really. He kept it all close to his chest. I only had the vaguest idea of what he got up to. He had this other life, you see, this separate existence. It was difficult living with him sometimes. He could be cold, detached, Mel, when the mood suited him. Grayling kept asking about the time he spent in Somerset but I told him I didn't know him then, how could I know about that? He never really talked much about it. That was in the past for Monty."

"Things didn't go well for Monty there, I believe?" asked Bottrell.

"You know about that? Of course he was much younger then and fairly influential in the pagan movement. But then it all started to change for him."

"How exactly?"

"He'd wanted to set up this foundation in memory of Gerald Gardner. It was to be a living memorial, that was the idea, that's how he described it to me. But he needed money to fund it – lots of it. He said he'd wanted it to be an international centre for witchcraft studies."

"So what happened to prevent it?" asked Bottrell.

"There was a problem with several of the sponsors. Some of them were dyed in the wool wiccans. They didn't much care for Monty's particular brand of magic. So they withdrew their support and the venture crashed. Monty was furious of course. He'd put his heart and soul into the venture. He was also being hounded by the tabloids. A Sunday paper had run this story about the centre being a cover for Black Magic rituals. Then of course there was the young girl who went missing. That made matters worse for him."

Bottrell put down his glass.

"Tell me about the girl."

"She was the daughter of a family who attended one of the big rituals there. She just disappeared. Of course it had nothing whatever to do with Monty, but you know what the press are like once they get their teeth into a

A Cromer Corpse

story. They just don't let go. There were all sorts of wild accusations – you know the sort of thing. Human sacrifice and the like. Monty did his best to ignore them. But they wouldn't let up. Kept the story running for weeks."

"And the police investigated it?"

"Yes, they interviewed a number of people – including Monty and Helen of course – but the child wasn't found. She probably simply ran away. Monty said the parents were peculiar anyway. The father was a known coke addict. They came down from Bristol I believe."

"Should think he was glad to move east," Melanie observed.

"Yes, it was a new start for him and Helen. Who'd have thought, though, five years later…"

Suddenly her face changed and her eyes filled with tears. Melanie put her arm round her. "It's okay," she said.

When Melanie drove Margaret back to the Watch House, Bottrell sat over a glass of brandy, smoking his briar. The image of the dead girl on the hill kept floating back into his befuddled brain. Could the missing girl in Somerset be a mere coincidence? Or had Druitt been some kind of crazed occultist? In the twenty first century nobody really practised human sacrifice. But once they did… The Celts did. There had been the bodies found in peat bogs, victims of ritual sacrifice. But was Druitt really capable of such a thing?

He finished his pipe, drew back the lounge curtains and stared out through the window. Although late, it was still not quite dark. The sun, now low on the horizon, threw a golden light across a calm and unruffled sea. In the foreground, the sand dunes, cast in shadow, appeared almost animate, like the bodies of strange, primeval beasts. Far off, in the distance, he could make out a sea

A Cromer Corpse

bird's keening cry. Finding the eeriness and isolation of the landscape almost overwhelming, he drew the curtains again and made his way into the kitchen where he poured himself another drink.

* * *

Earlsham was a small market town to the north of Norwich. Although it still boasted a number of fine Georgian buildings in its centre, the outlying areas had given way to sprawling housing estates where one row of houses looked much the same as another. Number 57, Wilberforce Avenue, lay in the middle of a block of drab terraced properties hastily constructed in the early '60's. Grayling parked the car by the edge of a scruffy green where derelict children's play equipment lay surrounded by an assortment of empty take away wrappings and lager cans.

"Nice neighbourhood, sir," murmured Waverley as they approached the property, but Grayling said nothing. He hated jobs like this. There was one thing worse than investigating the murder of a child and that was dealing with the bereaved parents. He had been through the ordeal twice before in his career and on each occasion he hadn't handled it well. Outwardly he had been fine but inwardly he had wept with them, shared the overwhelming sense of grief and loss they had experienced. At this moment he would rather have been anywhere than here. But he wasn't going to share that information with Simpson.

There was a sound of barking, then the door opened. A short, pale-faced woman in jeans and a blue t - shirt

A Cromer Corpse

bearing the legend "The Damned", stood in the doorway, her eyes full of sadness.

"Yes?"

Grayling and Waverley showed their warrant cards.

"Chief Inspector Grayling. Mrs Andrea Barnham?"

"Yes."

"My colleague telephoned earlier. We've come about your daughter. Wondered if we could have a word?"

The woman led the way down a long, sterile hallway where the flock wallpaper had turned a sickly yellow from decades of smoking.

"Just a minute," she said as they approached the kitchen door. "My dog."

More barking, the woman's raised voice, then silence. Andrea Banham re-emerged, a freshly lit cigarette hanging from her lower lip.

"Coffee?" she asked.

"White, with two sugars. Twice. Thanks."

She pointed to the lounge.

"I'll be a minute. Make yourselves comfortable."

Comfortable wasn't the right word. Grayling and Waverley sat on an imitation black leather sofa, staring at the large, barely furnished room. In one corner stood a cheap pine drinks cabinet, in the other a bookcase containing a pile of women's magazines and several framed photos. Grayling stood up to examine them. One in particular caught his interest. It showed a slim, blonde girl sitting on a swing. Unlike her mother, whom she vaguely resembled, her face was bright, intelligent. The photo had captured a moment of pure joy and abandonment, the face radiating pleasure. He picked it up.

"That's my Annie," said a voice behind him. He turned to face Mrs Banham, who was standing holding the tea tray, her face rigid and mask-like. She put down the tray and tapped her cigarette into a large black

A Cromer Corpse

ashtray. "It was taken about a month before she disappeared. We'd been on holiday to Dumfries."

"This was before your husband left you?"

"Look. Why have you come? Have you had news of her?"

Grayling handed back the photo. "You've not heard from your husband since then?" he asked, avoiding the plea.

"Not since a year ago. Why do you ask?"

"Mrs Banham, on the evening your daughter disappeared, can you recall what shoes she was wearing?"

"Trainers. White and blue trainers."

Simpson produced a photo. "Like these?"

There was a prolonged silence as the woman stared at the photo. Grayling watched her as the full horror of the realisation set in and her eyes filled with tears.

"Those are hers," she said at last, in a faltering voice.

"You're sure?"

"I'm certain. They were expensive. Her father bought them for her the day before…before she went missing. It had been her birthday. Where did you find them?"

"They were found on the body of a young girl."

"Where?"

"On Marston Hill. We made the discovery only yesterday."

Mrs Banham inhaled on her cigarette. Waverley could see she was shaking.

"I want to see her. When can I see her?"

"That's probably not a good idea," said Waverley. "We're checking dental records at the moment. She had been there a long time…"

"Mrs Banham, can you think of a reason why Annie might have gone to Morton? Did she have a friend there, for example?" asked Grayling.

"She had a friend who lived in Monkhampton – no one in Morton."

A Cromer Corpse

"And your husband. Did he have any connection with the place?"

"He did some building work there sometimes. Otherwise, no."

"I need to ask you this. Did your husband ever mistreat Annie in any way?"

"No, never. He used to knock me around – when he was drunk. But never Annie. They were close."

"When he left, he didn't leave a note – by way of explanation?"

"No, nothing. That was what was so hard to take. He left for work in the morning and Annie never came back from school. It all happened that one day. I thought he'd done it to spite me. Taken her, I mean. I said all this to the woman police officer at the time. Why ask me again?" There was a pause as Grayling finished his drink. "You're sure it's Annie?"

"We won't be absolutely certain until some tests are conducted. But it does seem likely. I'm extremely sorry Mrs Banham. I wondered – before we go – might it be possible to look at Annie's room?"

"Go ahead. It's the bedroom on the left at the top of the stairs. It hasn't been touched since Annie- "

Grayling opened the door to the small bedroom. Pop posters on the wall, a selection of furry toy animals on the window ledge, a small wardrobe and dressing table. On the dressing table some cheap jewellery and two framed photos, one showing Annie and her parents at what looked like a birthday celebration, the other, Annie with a boy and girl, slightly older than her, dressed as Goths. Grayling noticed that both youths had large silver pentacles hanging from their necks. There were no other clues, no diary, nothing more to indicate the personality of the girl. He picked up the photo and made his way downstairs.

"Mrs Banham, could you tell me who these young people are?" he asked.

A Cromer Corpse

CHAPTER NINE

The following summer, when she was thirteen, she returned to the wood and found the hut again. She had good cause to remember that summer for it was the time when her periods had begun in earnest. The coming of her periods marked a time of change and sorrow for her. Overnight, it seemed, everything about her had begun to shrink. Things she had once regarded as magical now seemed merely mundane. A grey cloak had descended over her world and it refused to budge.

She still held onto her collection of dolls, of course, but it was not the same. She no longer spoke to them, offered them her secrets, except, that is, for rag doll. Rag doll was special for Uncle had given it to her. And Uncle. He was special too. Special, that is, until the day came when she found out what was really in the hut in the woods.

That summer solstice it had been hotter than ever and the crowds who attended the festival bigger than before. There had also been a new group at the bonfires. New age travellers, some of whom were benign, others who were unpleasant and, when drunk, abusive. She had been glad, therefore, when dawn came at last, the dawn of midsummer's day. She determined to rise early and go into the woods.

6am. A heavy dew on the grass. Tents and litter, picked out by the early sunlight. She put on the floral dress her mother had given her for her birthday and,

A Cromer Corpse

slipping out of the small bedroom in the attic, made her way down the great oak staircase, out onto the verandah. Heavy in the air was the smell of last night's bonfire.

She made her way along the drive, heading for the woods. As she reached the footpath, the tall beeches and massive oaks gave shade from the midsummer sun. She remembered the path well. She had been along here the previous year when she had found the hut in the woods. At the end of the path she stopped, spotting a flash of colour amid the trees ahead. There was a sound of rustling leaves. Then she saw it: a young deer, head bent, half concealed between two giant ash trees. She waited, thinking she might be invisible to the creature, but the deer saw her, raised its head, then was off.

She continued onwards. After some five minutes she found the clearing and in its midst, the hut. Being a little taller than on her previous visit, she stood on tiptoe and tried peering in through the dusty curtains, but it was no use. They were drawn tight. From her pocket she took out the small Swiss penknife her father had given her as a present. One of the blades was thin and pointed, rather like a screwdriver. With this she started to work on the padlock which secured the door. To her surprise there was a sudden click and the hasp shifted. Removing the padlock, she pushed the door open.

Although dark inside, she could make out several objects standing on a low pine table and, around the walls of the hut, a series of bookshelves containing bottles and books. "Uncle's secret lair," she thought to herself. Her eyes now grown accustomed to the light, she stepped forward to examine the contents of the table. Two large black candle holders with beeswax candles, a leather bound book and an incense burner of the type used in old churches. But it was not these things which

A Cromer Corpse

fixed her attention and made her shiver with sudden fear. It was the sight of a large glass jar, a kilner jar like her mother used in the kitchen at home. Inside it and stuck through with long brass pins, was a bloody heart. Was it a human heart or the heart of an animal? She didn't know which.

Her heart beating fast, she drew back and turned to leave, but in so doing knocked the table. The jar toppled, then crashed to the floor, smashing into a dozen pieces. There followed an overwhelming smell of spirit. Then, without warning, something caught her eye, even more horrible than the thing she had seen on the table.

Hanging from a corner of the room, its legs suspended by a piece of string, was a crow. It twisted and turned this way and that, its beak opening and shutting. Through its dark breast ran a long silver needle. Someone had hung it there, crucified it, left it to slowly die. She opened her mouth to scream, but as she did so, a hand touched her shoulder and she spun round. It was Uncle, his face black as thunder.

A Cromer Corpse

CHAPTER TEN

By 9am the following morning the incident room at Norwich Central Police HQ was already full. Bottrell, who was sitting nursing a mug of black coffee and a headache in the front row, had been rung late the previous evening, hence his attendance.

"Charles here. I wonder if you could do me a favour, John?"

"About the Druitt case?"

"About the Druitt case. We've removed quite a bit of correspondence and a PC from Druitt's house. Plus some books on the occult and a diary he kept. I'd like you to look through the contents of the books and the diary, give me your expert opinion as it were. Okay with that?"

"Fine. What about the girl?"

"We talked to the mother yesterday. Not much to go on, though the father disappeared at the time the girl went missing."

"And where is he now?"

"We're trying to establish his whereabouts. We've made contact with the police in Dumfriesshire – his last known location, but nothing yet. However, there may be a connection with an occult group. It's a tenuous link though. I'll tell you more when I see you next. Can you attend a briefing – 9am tomorrow at HQ?"

Bottrell sipped his coffee, which he found acrid and bitter. His mind drifted back to former times when he had sat in rooms similar to this during his years in the Met. The bleak, overhead lighting, the uncomfortable plastic chairs, the buzz of conversation, the jokes about

A Cromer Corpse

absent colleagues, the sweating DC. Scribbling with marker pen on the large whiteboard, followed by the expectant hush as order descended. The only difference then had been the smoke filled room. Instinctively on entering he had reached into his jacket pocket and grasped the bowl of his briar, then remembering the Puritanism of the age, had withdrawn his hand. His reverie was interrupted by Grayling calling the meeting to order.

"Okay ladies and gentlemen, let's get on with it. You've already got my briefing notes about why you're all here so I don't want to waste time on that. As you know, we have two murders to investigate. It is a possibility – I stress, *only* a possibility at this stage – that they may in some way be linked. DC Waverley, give us the main facts please."

Bottrell looked at Waverley. Young, earnest, attractive, neatly dressed, probably from a university background. How things had changed.

"Montague Druitt. Body found by fishermen two days ago off Cromer. He'd been drugged with a barbiturate – probably amobarbital. Cause of death, drowning. Corpse had been mutilated post mortem. The tongue removed, head badly beaten. Also –", pointing to the whiteboard – "the pubic hair had been shaved off, When, we don't know. And a pentacle carved into the abdomen, here. This might suggest some sort of revenge or even ritual killing."

"We're attaching some significance to the pentacle," interrupted Grayling, "since we know Druitt had been a leading member of the pagan movement before he settled in Norfolk. He operated from a large house in Somerset where he organised meetings and festivals. It's possible the murderer might have a connection with that period in his life."

"Druitt's car was discovered near dunes at Morton," Waverley continued. "From the forensic evidence we're

A Cromer Corpse

sure he was attacked by two individuals – one taller and bigger than the other. However, there may have been a time gap before he was drowned. We're uncertain of the exact duration and of what happened to the victim during that time. Whoever did dump the body at sea took the precaution of weighing down the victim's trousers with coins – but clearly not thoroughly enough."

Grayling stepped forward to the screen.

"Okay. Thanks, DC Waverley. Now. Suspects. Druitt lived with a woman called Margaret Jones. They ran an occult bookshop in Morton. He was estranged from his wife Helen, who also lives locally. According to Jones, Druitt had received hate mail from Helen. She also claims someone had interfered with their car's brakes but Druitt never reported this to the police. We have some letters Jones had been sent by Helen Druitt but since she claimed Druitt destroyed his letters her evidence is at best circumstantial. Nonetheless Helen Druitt remains a suspect. But who is the accomplice? At present we have nothing on that. Yesterday Simpson and I removed a quantity of Druitt's correspondence plus a PC from his house and I want you lot to check the stuff out. By that I mean Rankin and Waverley." Rankin, a small, pale faced Scot, nodded from the side of the room. Although Grayling had worked with Rankin for years, Rankin had never quite lost that suggestion of anxiety which seemed to hover about him permanently. Though ruthlessly efficient, Rankin always gave the air of a man who was overwhelmed by events.

"You'll be assisted by my ex colleague, John Bottrell. I haven't formally introduced John. He's an old colleague of mine from the Met, now retired, but he has some expertise in matters relating to occult groups. Some of you may remember him from the Zennor murder case." Heads nodded. Someone at the back started to clap. Grayling gave him a withering look, then

A Cromer Corpse

continued. "It's likely, given the evidence, that the accomplice lives locally, so I want you to keep your options open. Find out what Druitt's contacts were in the area. Remember, the occult connection may well provide us with the key to this business. Which leads us to our second murder."

Grayling sat down and Waverley continued.

"Right. Second victim is Annie Banham. Lived with parent – mother – in Earlsham. Anne disappeared last summer whilst on her way back from school. This coincided with the disappearance of her father Michael. We've checked with the force north of the border in Dumfries where he was last spotted but as yet no clue to his whereabouts. The body was found near Morton Wood in a shallow grave by archaeologists. Pathologist estimates time of death near to or on Midsummer's Day a year ago. Because of the sandy soil the body had been well preserved – mummified. Cause of death: strangulation though she'd been struck on the back of the head with a blunt object, possibly a stone or flint axe. She'd also imbibed a herbal potion consisting of hemlock and valerian. Effect: part poison, part anaesthetic. Because of the position of the burial and these factors I've mentioned it seems possible that her death was of a ritual nature."

"Anybody any questions?" Grayling asked as Waverley sat down. Someone raised his hand.

"So what are we saying, then? That these two deaths were part of some linked ritual?"

"No, we aren't assuming that. At this stage the connection is at best tenuous. One factor came to light yesterday regarding the girl though. She had a couple of school friends who were Goths. We'll be interviewing them tomorrow to see if there's some kind of connection. There is one other factor which may have relevance. When Druitt was in Somerset a young girl

A Cromer Corpse

who attended one of the festivals there went missing. She was never found despite an extensive investigation."

"So what – Druitt may have been a paedophile?" someone else asked.

"We have no direct evidence he was – yet. And Annie Banham was not molested. Our best option is to find the father. As regards Druitt, we need to find some link in his past which might give us a clue as to the murderer's motive. John already has some data on his former life in Somerset. Let's hope the stuff from his house can give us more. There's also the local angle we need to look at. For example, he was friendly with two antique dealers in Morton: Bradley Evans and Alex Smith. He also knew a local fisherman, Peter Riscorla. We know that Druitt went on a short break to Amsterdam last year with Riscorla and according to Margaret Jones that's where he told her he was bound for on the evening she last saw him. He said he was visiting someone on business there but didn't tell her who. We therefore need to find out who this person was. I'll be interviewing the school kids this afternoon but until then we have the morning to shape things up. If there are no more questions then, let's get on with it."

* * *

As he climbed the hill, he became aware of a sound: a slow, insistent, drumming. coming up from the direction of the wood. He looked up. Already the sun was low on the horizon, the sky turning from blue to orange to red as sunset fast approached.

It was the midsummer solstice. He looked down at the clothes he was wearing. A long, hessian cloak, pulled in at the middle by a leather belt. His trousers were a dark plaid, rough and coarse to the touch. Around his neck,

A Cromer Corpse

attached by a leather thong, was a silver pendant in the shape of a horse.

The drumming was much louder now and he could smell the fire. Beyond the top of the trees he could see the smoke billowing. As he continued his climb upwards, he could make out a large company of people standing in a circle near the burial mound. Some drummed, others chanted or danced.

The sun was almost near the horizon line now and the air at his back had grown suddenly colder. He sat down on a fallen tree trunk and watched. The drumming abruptly ceased. One by one, the assembly drew back, then sank to their knees. From a gap in the trees three figures emerged, dressed in white, each bearing the insignia of the horse goddess. The tallest of the three, who held a white staff, stood by the fire, facing the sun, and began to chant.

Then he saw the girl. Robed in dark green, she emerged from the trees. Her hair had been festooned with flowers and her hands were bound with twine. She would have been no more than thirteen he guessed.

The circle of people were on their feet now, joining hands, moving to left and right, a low chant rising up on the still, warm air. He watched as the white robed figures surrounded the girl. One began to ululate, then, raising a long hafted stone axe, brought it down heavily on the head of the girl…

* * *

A Cromer Corpse

He woke suddenly, the dream still vivid, but already starting to fade from his mind. Beside him lay Melanie, sleeping. It was already growing light. He slipped out of bed and sat on the bedside chair for a moment, clutching his head. He had experienced dreams of such clarity before, he told himself, many times. This was surely nothing new. The ability to connect with the unseen world was something he had inherited from his mother. It was not something he often talked about except to Melanie. In the past, though, it had occasionally been useful to him. On this occasion he wasn't so sure. Was it just the result of an over-active imagination or had he really glimpsed some kind of ritual which had taken place on that hill centuries ago? Or maybe even a year ago?

Putting on his dressing gown, he slipped downstairs to the kitchen and began making himself a mug of coca. Soon the smell of warm milk began to fill the room. Through the kitchen door he could just glimpse the sky, turning from red to yellow as the sun gradually ascended. He poured the milk into the mug, added the cocoa, then went into the lounge. Reaching for his briar, he filled and lit it, then sat in the wicker chair, turning over the two murders in his mind. Was there really some sort of magical connection or was the girl's murder unconnected? And had Druitt's past finally caught up with him? Or had he been murdered by someone close to him? Helen Druitt perhaps?

On the table by the CD player sat the two boxes of correspondence marked "evidence" Grayling had given him to pour over. Tomorrow he would give it his full attention. But for now he had his cocoa, his pipe and the silence of the dawn to contemplate. Lying back in the chair, he inhaled deeply, then watched as a plume of smoke curled upwards towards the ceiling. He was

A Cromer Corpse

thinking not of Druitt but of Frances and of better times, long ago, in Cornwall.

* * *

John and Abigail Stevenson lived in a small village to the east of Earlsham. Once a prosperous community, in recent years Earlsham had declined dramatically, partly because of the influx of second home owners from Essex and Cambridgeshire, but mainly because of the construction of a large hypermarket on the edge of the village.

The Stevenson twins lived with their mother, Julia, in a small, two-bedroomed cottage adjacent to the village church. Their father, James, had left the family several years ago, leaving their mother as sole breadwinner.

Grayling yawned and scratched his head. This was followed by the realisation that his hair was unwashed and slightly greasy. Living alone, DCI Grayling often took little stock of the finer points of sartorial correctness, often turning up to work in a creased suit or, on some occasions, tieless. By contrast, DC Waverley, his assistant this bright summer morning, was neatly dressed with coiffured hair and a hint of patchouli oil which Grayling found faintly arousing. Not a chance, he thought. She's twice your age.

It was John Stevenson who answered the door to them. Just over six feet in height, pale and aquiline faced with dyed black hair, his appearance was made even more severe by his black, collarless jacket and large, ankle length, studded boots.

A Cromer Corpse

"Yes? What do you want?" he snapped at them, imperiously.

Grayling showed his warrant card.

"I'm Chief Inspector Grayling and this is DC Waverley. Is your mother in?"

"She's working. Why?"

"It's you we've come to see. And your sister."

"You'd better come in then I suppose."

He turned and shouted down the hall: "Abi! Abi! It's the Bill!" They passed down a narrow hallway into a dilapidated lounge, furnished with a battered sofa and two wicker chairs, painted a vivid, bilious green. Grayling detected a faint smell of cannabis in the air, a suspicion which was confirmed by an ash tray on the coffee table containing several over-sized cigarette butts.

He sat down on the sofa and waited as Waverley stood awkwardly, looking out of the lounge window. John Stevenson left the room in search of his sister.

"Smell that?" asked Grayling.

"I smell it sir."

He stared at the poster on the wall. It was a black and white still from one of those old silent films, showing a bald headed ghoul with long, talon-like fingernails, bent over the sleeping body of a young woman. Below the photo was the single word: "Nosferatu."

"Nice view?"

"It's the back of the churchyard."

Abigail Stevenson entered the room. She bore a striking resemblance to her brother but her face, unlike his, was ethereal, with dark brown eyes and full, sensuous lips which she had painted crimson. She must have been scarcely seventeen, Grayling conjectured, but looked much older.

"What's this all about?" she asked, sitting down opposite Grayling and Waverley.

A Cromer Corpse

"It's about Annie Banham," Grayling replied. "You both knew her I believe?"

John glanced at his sister before replying.

"We knew her. She was at Earlsham School in our last year there."

"How well did you know her?"

"Annie was a bright kid," said Abigail, avoiding the question. "Not like the usual thirteen year old. She was into all sorts of stuff."

"Like what?" asked Waverley.

"Things alternative and spiritual," John Stevenson replied. "She was unique for a girl her age."

"She latched herself onto John," interrupted Abigail. "At first I thought she was a bit freaky. But once we got to know her it was okay. She turned up at one of the pagan moots in Norwich. That's where we first met her. She was very earnest. Into saving the planet – that kind of stuff."

"And what kind of stuff are you into, Abigail?" asked Waverley.

"The Northern Tradition."

"And what's that?" asked Grayling.

"We follow the old gods from Northern Mythology, inspector. Principally Odin and Freya."

"And Annie. She shared these interests did she?"

"She showed some interest in our beliefs, yes, you could say that. But she had her own beliefs."

"And what were they?"

"I can't rightly say. She liked the music. She used to tag along with us to gigs."

"What about her mum?" asked Waverley. "Didn't she mind?"

"She used to come to the gigs with an older friend – Susan Blight , or one of the others in year ten. She was old for her age, and wiser than a lot of other thirteen year olds. Sometimes we'd give her a lift back in the

A Cromer Corpse

camper van. Sometimes she made her own way back. It varied."

"Okay," said Grayling. "I want to ask you both about June 21st last year."

John Stevenson smiled.

"You mean the midsummer solstice?" What of it?"

"Can you account for your movements on that day?"

"We went through all this a year ago," said Abigail. "It's the day Annie disappeared, isn't it?"

"Right. But I want you to go through it again."

John Stevenson sat down in the chair opposite Grayling and Waverley, his arms folded. "Okay then. We were both at school that day. Then we went home, had a meal. In the evening we went to Blackling Hall to the concert. Black Sabbat – a tribute group – were playing there. We got there around – what – six thirty?"

"Six thirty," Abigail confirmed.

"Early enough to get through the fence on the wooded side of the estate. We'd arranged to meet Annie and Susan Blight by the west entrance once we got in but she never showed. We hung around for about half an hour, then gave up."

"And what time did you leave the concert?"

John Stevenson glanced at his sister.

"Dunno – around midnight or so?"

"And you didn't think it odd she hadn't turned up? Didn't think of letting her mother know?"

Stevenson smiled. "Annie was a free spirit, Inspector. But of course, I was forgetting, you wouldn't know about that, would you? You didn't know her."

"No, but you did," rejoined Grayling. "You mentioned she attended a pagan meeting in Norwich. Was she a member? Did she do that on a regular basis?"

"I don't know that she was a member. She was interested in witchcraft of course. There was a small group of them in her year – all girls – who were. Susan Blight was one of them. Annie and Susie used to get

A Cromer Corpse

together at each others' houses and do stuff. I'm not entirely sure how serious it all was."

"Tell me, do you recognise this man?" Grayling asked, producing a photo of Druitt. John Stevenson passed the photo to his sister who stared at it.

"The face is familiar," said John.

Abigail nodded. "He came to one or two of the moots a couple of years back. Haven't seen him for a long while though. Isn't he the guy -?"

"Yes, his body was found in the sea near Cromer a few days ago."

"How well did you know him?" asked Waverley.

"We didn't," said Abigail. "We only met him a few times. Struck me as something of a loner. As if he'd come to the meetings to watch us. I found that a bit creepy if you want the truth."

"Was he there when Annie went to the meetings?"

"I don't recall. He might have been. There were a lot of people there at that time."

"Did you speak to him?"

"I spoke to him once – briefly," said John.

"And what did you talk about?" asked Grayling.

"This and that. He seemed interested in the Gothic. We talked a bit about the Northern Tradition. He was interested in the Odinic rites. I remember now."

"The what?"

"The Odinic rites. The rituals associated with Odin. They're mentioned by some of the Roman writers in classical times."

"And these rituals – what do they involve?"

"Sacrifice to the God."

"Human sacrifice?"

"So the classical writers would have it – yes."

"What, like in the film, The Wicker Man?"

"Well, that's a bit far-fetched really. But yes, that sort of thing may have taken place. We don't really have the evidence to prove it either way."

A Cromer Corpse

"Did Druitt talk about anything else to you?"

"Told me he ran a bookshop in Morton. Suggested I might be interested in some of the rare editions he stocked. I told him I had no money."

Just then there was a sound of a key turning in the front door. A woman appeared at the doorway to the lounge. She wore a long red dress and had a shock of curly red hair. Her face was long and drawn, her eyes a deep green. Grayling detected a strong odour of incense about her. She put down the shopping bag she was holding and stared at the detectives.

"What's going on, John?" she asked.

"These people are detectives. They've come to ask us about Annie Banham."

After they left the house, Grayling sat with Waverley in the car in silence for a while. Then Waverley said: "D'you think they were telling us the truth, sir?"

"Some of it, yes. But I'm not sure about the connection with Druitt. I get the distinct feeling it was more than a casual acquaintance. I'd like to talk to this girl Susan Blight – hear what she has to say. Did you notice how wary the mother was? Almost as if she was hiding something. Question is: what? If Druitt was connected to these two, they may have procured the child for him. The boy has a knowingness to him. But not just that. He's cold, detached. I just get this feeling…" Waverley didn't reply. The appalling vision of Annie Banham's sacrifice as part of some blood ritual had filled her mind.

"Anyway, we'll need to check the CCTV footage for Blackling Hall. That is, if they haven't already done so. We need to know if the girl did or didn't turn up to the concert. We need to get at the truth."

"You don't think the father was involved then?"

"We got an email from Dumfries police just before we left. I forgot to tell you. They confirmed that Michael

A Cromer Corpse

Banham was involved in a public disorder in Dumfries on the night after Annie went missing. He was cautioned but released. After that they lost track of him. No, I think we can probably eliminate Michael Banham from our enquiries. I'm convinced they key to this one lies with Druitt. And we can't ask him."

"Dead men tell no tales," Waverley replied.

Grayling smiled, then turned the ignition key. Soon the car was speeding through Earlsham Village in the direction of Norwich. What was it about that patchouli oil, he wondered?

A Cromer Corpse

CHAPTER ELEVEN

Peter Riscorla found the office in a small back street off Bestervaerstraat in the north sector of Amsterdam. It had been a hot journey. The small plane from Norwich had been packed because it was the height of the holiday season and the interior of the cabin was claustrophobic and humid. When he finally arrived at Schipol airport, conditions were not much better. He had difficulty finding his luggage and taxis were scarce. Eventually he decided to walk from the rail station, relying on the street map Druitt had given him.

There were three names on the intercom. Riscorla pressed the top one, marked "Jan Van Verhoeven" and waited momentarily as sweat trickled down the back of his neck. A voice answered. Since Riscorla had no Dutch he gave his name in English and the door opened, admitting him into a narrow hallway with dingy brown walls and a faint smell of tobacco.

Climbing the stairs, he found a door on the first landing marked "Van Verhoeven" and knocked gently. A black colossus in a grey suit opened the door. "Mr Van Verhoeven will see you in a minute. Sit here and wait." Though the man spoke perfect English there was something about his tone which made Riscorla uneasy. He looked at the man's hands which were large and spatulate. He was built like a wrestler and smelt of cheap cologne. Riscorla did as he was told and sat opposite a large poster displaying an Amazonian woman with pendulous breasts. After a short while the colossus

A Cromer Corpse

returned. "Mr Van Verhoeven will now see you," he instructed.

Van Verhoeven was a short, stocky man with cropped blonde hair. He was immaculately dressed in a dark, charcoal suit, lilac shirt and matching tie and smoked a cigar. When he smiled at Riscorla, his white teeth gleamed. A man of expensive tastes, Riscorla thought.

"Sit down, Mr Riscorla, sit down. I was distressed to hear of your colleague's misfortune. Of course, I read of it in the English papers. It saddened me, though, Mr Riscorla, that you did not think it proper to inform me personally of the death of Mr Druitt."

There was a long pause as Van Verhoeven stared at him. Then he tapped the ash from his cigar impatiently into a glass ashtray. Riscorla didn't reply.

"Naturally, I assume your reticence had to do with the fact that Mr Druitt owed me money, Mr Riscorla. Quite a deal of money."

"How much?" asked Riscorla, shifting in his chair.

"The complete sum is just over sixty thousand euros. This is of course for the last consignment."

"The last consignment?"

"Come now, Mr Riscorla, there is no need to act the dumb fool with me."

Riscorla became aware of the close proximity of the colossus who was now standing behind his left shoulder.

"You were, I believe, part of the operation. You took the last consignment on board your vessel. That is correct, isn't it?" Riscorla remembered alright. He had picked up the consignment from a Dutch fishing vessel a week before Druitt's demise.

"That's true. So what – Monty never paid you? Is that it?"

"You have it right, Mr Riscorla. Hence my message to you asking you to come and explain this oversight. So where is the money I am owed?"

A Cromer Corpse
"I thought he'd paid you. I thought –"

"Then you thought wrong. In order that we continue doing business together, I must insist payment reaches me in the next five working days. A banker's draft will suffice. Hans here will give you the details before you leave. A failure to comply will lead to most unpleasant circumstances. Do I make myself abundantly clear?"

"Abundantly clear."

"Very well, then, by the 30th. Now, unless you have any other matter you wish to discuss with me, you are free to leave."

Outside, in the sultry city air, Riscorla stood for a moment, wondering what to do. In a dingy alleyway opposite, a hooded figure squatted, rocking gently, locked in an alcoholic trance. Suddenly the enormity of his situation began to overwhelm him. In an instant he knew what he must do.

* * *

After Melanie had left for work, Bottrell went downstairs, made himself a coffee, then stood in the lounge, staring out through the French windows. The sun was already high, casting its golden light over the dunes. Further off, to the north, he could make out a large flock of gulls wheeling above long stretches of deserted dunes. He opened the windows and stood outside for a while, listening to their mournful cries, feeling the cold easterly wind and thinking about the girl's body in the barrow on the hill. Was Grayling right and could there be a connection with Druitt? Was he truly capable of ritual murder? So far Grayling had been unable to establish a direct link between the two. Still, it was early days.

A Cromer Corpse

Finishing his coffee, he went back inside, grabbed his briar, and reached for the box Grayling had given him to examine. Inside, he found a large day to day diary, an account book and several volumes, one of which was leather bound and, judging by its appearance, of some antiquity. The title of the book was "Nygramancia", and, according to the title page, had originally been published in Munich in 1468. The volume he held in his hands appeared to be a rare reprint and had been produced in a limited edition of 100 copies in Berlin in 1787. Bottrell's Latin was rusty but adequate. Ignoring the other contents of the box, he reached for his pipe, then settled back in the wicker chair, perusing the volume's contents.

It appeared to be some sort of medieval grimoire, a collection of spells and magical formulae, in short, a necromancer's manual. The author was Johannes Cunalis, a priest of Munich. Bottrell could tell that the orthography was highly erratic and the Latin usage unconventional. It seemed that Cunalis was not the necromancer but simply the compiler of other mens' work. The book comprised formulae for commanding the spirits and experiments with divination. And there were also sections on the magic of circles and spheres. He started to read the first section:

*Nygramancia (*it began*) is the first forbidden art, and is called the black art. This art is the worst of all, because it proceeds with sacrifices and services that must be rendered to the Devils. One who wishes to exercise this art must give all sorts of sacrifices to the Devils and must make an oath and pact with them. Then the Devils are obedient to him and will carry out the will of the master. Take note of two great evils in this art. The first is the master must deny God and render divine honours to the Devils, for we should only make sacrifices to God,*

A Cromer Corpse
who redeemed us by his passion. The other is that he binds himself to the Devil, who is the great enemy of mankind.

Bottrell plugged his pipe, lit it, then placed the book on the table. He walked over to the window and looked out, smoke curling from the pipe's bowl. Could Druitt have been capable of human sacrifice or was his interest in dark magic purely academic? How serious was he in his commitment to this grimoire of a long forgotten age? The book itself could not stand as evidence of his involvement in Annie Banham's death. It amounted to nothing more than supposition. If there was a real link, then he wouldn't find it here between the pages of this musty volume.

He closed the book and put it back in the box. Next to it was a much smaller volume, bound in black with gilt lettering, entitled A Handbook Of Masonic Reference. He opened it. On the fly leaf was an inscription which read: "With fondest love from Bradley." For a moment he wondered about the name. Bradley. Bradley Evans. Of course. The antique dealer. He leafed through the pages. Then, at page 172, he paused. He was looking at a pentacle. Beneath it was this entry:

The Pentalpha or Five Pointed Star is a mysterious symbol of great antiquity, credited with magical powers. It was much used by the Pythagoreans but is probably much older. It was also much used by the medieval masons as a mark and is frequently found on the stones of old buildings. In Christian symbolism it is supposed to refer to the five wounds of Christ. Among Freemasons, the number five is an important one.

For a long while Bottrell sat with the book open at the page, staring at the pentacle. Then he finished his pipe,

A Cromer Corpse
picked up the phone and dialled Grayling's direct number.

* * *

What are you doing here?"

The voice was hard, the question demanding. This was not the quiet, soft spoken Uncle she had grown to know and the face, with its furrowed brows and curled lip, was not his, either. He towered above her, arms folded, looking down on her, eyes pinpoints of fury.

She opened her mouth to reply but found she was unable to do so. Her left hand opened involuntarily and she dropped the rag doll on the dusty floor. All around her, in the dark hut, was the smell of death and decay, and in the eyes of her inquisitor were pools of darkness.
"I wanted to know – to know what was inside," she blurted out.
"How long have you been here?"
"Not long. I just came."
"Do your parents know you're here?"
"No."
"You've been here before?"
"Only once. I looked through the window. What is this place?"

Uncle folded his arms. He turned to the open door, shut it, then beckoned her to a corner of the room. When he turned back to face her, he was smiling and his voice was softer. He pulled out two small fold up chairs.
"Sit down here for a while," he said, picking up the rag doll and gently dusting it. He handed it to her. "We need

A Cromer Corpse

to have a little chat, I think," he said, sitting opposite her.

"What is this place?"

Her heart was slowing now and she had stopped shaking. Uncle reached for her hand and grasped it. He was his old kind self again and the other person she had momentarily glimpsed had slipped back into the shadows. He smiled at her again, his white teeth gleaming in the shaft of sunlight that now penetrated the dark interior of the hut.

"This is my magic, secret place. It's where I do things. Where I contact the spirits."

"You mean the faeries?"

"Yes, the faeries. And other folk of the invisible world. Do you know what I mean by that?"

"Yes."

"And this is the place I come to when I need peace and quiet."

"But these things – these dead things –"

"Things I've found in the woods. I bring them here and give them healing. Sometimes I bring them back to life again. Sometimes I'm not able to do that. But I always try, for they're all creatures of the Goddess. Listen to me. You mustn't tell anyone you've been here. This must be our secret. If you dare tell anyone, anyone at all, including your mum and dad, this place will lose its power and we will neither of us ever see the invisible creatures of the woods. Never again. Do you understand?"

She nodded.

"I understand."

"Now," said Uncle, standing up, "what about a drink? A cup of tea."

She sat, holding rag doll as Uncle boiled a kettle over a small primus stove, thinking about the spirits of the

A Cromer Corpse

wood and what he had said about keeping a secret. Of course he was right to be angry. She understood now.

She drank the tea, which seemed strangely bitter. Feeling immensely sleepy, she lay back in the chair, listening to Uncle's soft voice as he chatted to her. Soon she was fast asleep.

When she awoke, she found herself sitting under a large oak tree near the perimeter of the wood. Her head ached and she felt cold, despite the heat of the day. As she stood up she swayed slightly and had to steady herself by holding onto the branch of the tree. Her mouth was dry and had a bitter taste.

She found the footpath and began walking back to the house, aware that the sun was higher now in the sky. When she cleared the trees, she looked down at the skirt she was wearing. It was badly creased as if it had been crumpled beneath her. And there was something else, an odour to her body that wasn't hers. When she finally reached the house she went to her bedroom and washed.

A Cromer Corpse

CHAPTER TWELVE

Alex Smith and Bradley Evans had only just arrived at Morton Antiques when the door-bell rang. A red-faced Alex made his way slowly downstairs to find two thick-set men in dark suits staring at him through the shop door. The older of the two men held a warrant card and was gesticulating. Alex rubbed his tousled hair and sighed. Police. What were they doing ringing the bell at this time of the morning?

Alex and Bradley were recovering from a late night's carousing. They had spent the evening at the Flamingo, a small night club off the Price of Wales Road in Norwich and a well known resort for gay men. The event, billed as a "fetish night," had been a popular venue, attracting as many as two hundred men from the surrounding area. Alex and Bradley had arrived early and had been pleasantly surprised at the large number of attractive younger men in attendance.

Not long after the Dutch bondage group had got under way, Alex had disappeared to the bar, leaving a disgruntled Bradley alone at their table and had spent the rest of the night chatting up a tall blonde youth who turned out to be a body builder from Great Yarmouth. Bradley, who was ten years older than his partner, had not been surprised at this development. Alex, the more promiscuous of the two, often made a habit of this sort of thing. In the early days of their relationship such incidents had led to blazing rows between them but in recent years Bradley had developed a quiet resignation. A sower of wild oats, Alex always returned to him in the

A Cromer Corpse

end. It was as if such infidelities only served to strengthen their often torrid relationship.

    Cursing under his breath, Alex drew back the bolts, turned the closed sign over and opened the door.
"Yes?"
"Police. I'm Inspector Grayling and this is DC Waverley. Are you Alex Smith?"
"What's this about?" came a voice from behind Alex. The two policemen stared at the stocky, balding figure in the towelling robe standing behind the younger man. Though older, he was well preserved and possessed an aristocratic face, lined with the vicissitudes of a chaotic and often tragic life.
"I'm Alex Smith," replied the younger man.
"We need to speak to you about Montague Druitt."
"Then you'd best come in," said Evans.

* * *

The moment that Margaret Jones reached the threshold of the Ariel Bookshop, she sensed something was amiss. The door lay ajar and it was clear that the lock had been forced, for there were splinters of wood protruding from the freshly painted frame. She entered gingerly, taking care not to touch anything in her path towards the office at the back of the shop. The piles of books which had decorated the office table lay untouched, an indication that whoever the intruder was, it was unlikely to have involved youthful vandals. She stood for a moment in the silent shop, listening, but it was soon clear that the burglar had long departed. Taking a mobile phone from her handbag, she dialled for the police.

A Cromer Corpse
* * *

"How well did you know Montague Druitt?" asked Charles Grayling.

The four men were sitting in the upstairs flat of the antique shop. Grayling and Waverley had taken up residence on a long, polka dot sofa, whilst opposite them, perched on a chaise longue, sat Evans and Smith. Waverley found herself staring at Evans' naked leg, which had slipped through his towelling robe.

"We both knew Monty, Inspector," rejoined Evans. "We knew him very well. We were friends of his. Had been for a long time."

"And fellow freemasons. Tell me more about that."

"Monty was Lodge Master here in Morton," Evans answered. "In fact he introduced us both to freemasonry."

"He'd been part of the Craft for some while?"

"Yes, I guess before he moved here to Norfolk. He was very well informed about it. Had a good deal of books on the subject and so on. I – we – were impressed by the depth of his knowledge."

"You say you were good friends. Exactly how close were you, Mr Smith?"

There was a slight pause. Alex blushed slightly.

"What do you mean exactly?"

"I mean was there ever a physical relationship with Druitt?"

"Certainly not."

"Then would you mind explaining the inscription in this book?" Grayling said, passing him the volume on freemasonry.

"Let me see that," interrupted Evans, snatching the volume from his partner's grasp and scanning the inscription. He looked at Smith, eyes blazing, then strode into the bedroom, slamming the door behind him.

A Cromer Corpse

"Look," said Smith, "this is a bit awkward. Could we discuss the matter in private?"

"By all means. You can come down to the station and continue the discussion there." Grayling stood up.

"What – now?"

"No time like the present."

"Just a minute then. I'll get my jacket."

Smith disappeared into the bedroom. Through the door the two policemen could hear raised voices. Smith emerged, face flushed. "Okay, I'm ready."

* * *

"Sit down here Margaret, and I'll get you a tea," said Melanie. Ashen-faced, Margaret Jones sat behind the antique pine desk while Bottrell cast a cursory glance round the bookshop's back office. "What have they taken?" he said at last.

"A number of antiquarian volumes from the cabinet. Oh and almost the entire contents of the safe."

"What was in it?"

"Cheque books – two – cash takings, a couple of credit cards, an account book and some letters."

"Have you contacted the banks?"

"Not yet. The cards were in Monty's name."

"We can get round that. You said almost the entire contents. What was left?"

"Some of Monty's diaries."

She pointed to a small pile of black volumes on the desk top.

"Mind if I have a look at these later?"

"I don't mind," she sighed.

"Did the shop have an alarm?"

"We do have one but it wasn't working. Monty had intended to have it fixed shortly before…"

A Cromer Corpse

Melanie entered, holding a tray with three mugs of coffee on it.

"The police will be here shortly," said Bottrell. "Meanwhile, try not to touch anything, Margaret."

He walked through into the hallway to examine the forced door. "Not a bad job," he said to himself quietly.

* * *

Inside interview room four, the air was close and oppressive. Alex Smith sat opposite Grayling and Waverley, hands clasped on the formica table. Grayling took out a packet of cigarettes and offered him one. He shook his head.

"I try not to," he said.

"Let me remind you, Mr Smith, this is an informal interview. You're not under caution."

"I understand."

"Tell us about your relationship with Montague Druitt."

Grayling leaned back in the chair, adopting a disarming attitude.

"I guess I'd known Monty for quite a few years. More or less since he moved here to Norfolk. We got to know each other through some antiques he bought from the shop."

"And for how long had you been lovers?"

"I didn't say we were."

"No, but you were, weren't you?"

"For a short while, yes."

"When exactly?"

"Quite recently."

"And your partner – Bradley – he knew of this relationship?"

A Cromer Corpse

"He suspected something was going on, yes. But he didn't suspect it was Monty."

"This relationship – did Monty's partner know about it?"

"He never mentioned she did."

"And where did these liaisons take place?"

"There was a room at the Lodge."

"The Freemason's Hall?"

"Yes. Monty and I both had keys. We used to go there on a Wednesday afternoon. I told Bradley I was at a health club in Norwich. Bradley and me were members of the club. Then, one day, he turned up there out of the blue and someone told him I hadn't been there for weeks."

"And you were still continuing this relationship up to the time of Druitt's disappearance?"

"Yes."

"When was the last time you saw each other?"

"A couple of nights before the Lodge meeting – the one he never turned up to. We met for a drink in Norwich. Monty said he was on his way to the airport to meet a guy in Amsterdam – a business contact of his."

"Did he say who this person was?"

"No. He kept the business side of his life quite private. Rarely mentioned it to me. Bradley was more involved with that side of things."

"In what way involved?"

"Bradley and Monty had known each other for years. Long before Monty moved here to Norfolk. They were both masons. That's how I got involved in the Craft."

"You say they'd known each other for years. Where was that?"

"In Somerset. Before Bradley got into freemasonry he was active on the pagan scene. He was part of a group which operated around Wells. Monty gave a talk at one of the regional conferences they had there and that's where they first met. Then, when Monty moved to the

A Cromer Corpse

big house in Somerset, Bradley and his group attended one of the celebrations. Then they both got involved in this scheme to set up a foundation."

"What was that?"

"It was an idea Monty had to set up a Wiccan trust in honour of the late Gerald Gardner."

"Gerald who?" asked Waverley.

"Gerald Gardner, the King of the Witches," said Grayling. "Go on."

"Monty set up this committee of thirteen people. The idea was each member would invest a certain sum of money into the foundation. Bradley put up quite a lot of his savings. But the whole thing collapsed. There were arguments about how the foundation should be run. Then the lease on the house came to an end, Monty ran out of money and finally he had to leave."

"What happened to the investors?"

"They lost the lot. It turned out afterwards Monty was up to his eyes in debt. Had been for a while."

"And Bradley – how did he react?"

"He was angry, understandably, but there was nothing he could do about it. Monty registered as a bankrupt. Then, when he got the chance of moving up here to Norfolk, he jumped at it. It was his wife who put up the money for the bookshop, not Monty."

"So how come Bradley remained on speaking terms with Monty?"

"He'd always admired Monty. Monty had this charisma, this way about him. It's difficult to explain if you've not met him."

"You say Bradley was owed money. How much money?"

"A lot. I'm not entirely sure."

"Thousands?"

"Yes, thousands, certainly."

"So surely he must have resented it?"

A Cromer Corpse

"As I said, he was angry but he forgave him. When Monty moved to Norfolk he gave Bradley some oil paintings he'd collected as a form of recompense. They were valuable pieces and he sold them at auction in Norwich. Got a good price for them. It helped heal the rift."

"You said Bradley was close to Monty. How close?" asked Waverley. Alex Smith stared back at her. "What do you mean?"

"I think you know what I mean."

"You're suggesting they had a physical relationship?"

"I'm suggesting that."

"I don't believe they did."

"Why not?" asked Grayling. "You said Bradley knew Druitt in Somerset. That was before you two got together, wasn't it?"

"Yes. But if it had happened, Bradley would have told me, I'm sure."

"Certain of that?"

"I'm certain, yes."

"Okay, that's probably all we need from you at the moment. There is one final thing I need to ask," said Grayling. "About Monty. Did he ever ask you to take part in a ritual?"

"No, never. Unless you include freemasonry in that definition."

"Did he talk about his magical beliefs to you?"

"Rarely. I knew he'd been a Wiccan of course when he'd lived in Somerset but it was Bradley who told me about that part of his life. Monty never really referred to it. It was part of his past, I guess."

"And he never asked you to participate in any magical ceremony?"

"No never. He was more interested in freemasonry."

"Tell me, do you recognise this girl?" asked Grayling, showing him the photo of Annie Banham. Alex looked at it.

A Cromer Corpse

"No, I don't. She's the murdered girl, isn't she? The one they found on the hill?"

"She is."

Alex Smith glanced at Waverley who was staring at him closely.

"Okay, Mr Smith, you can go. Thanks for your co-operation."

"Will you need to speak to Bradley?"

"Quite probably."

"I'd best get back. I've got some explaining to do."

Grayling smiled. He opened the interview room door and Smith left. Waverley noted that it was a smile tinged with contempt.

A Cromer Corpse

CHAPTER THIRTEEN

Some time in the early hours of the morning Margaret Jones woke. She had retired late after consuming too much red wine and her head felt drowsy from the effects of the alcohol. She had been dreaming again. It was a recurring dream. Since Monty's death she had experienced the dream with ever increasing clarity and she wondered why that was.

Throwing back the bedcovers, she went over to the window and peered out. It was already getting light and from here she could see a white mist enveloping the spit and the ocean beyond it. To her left she could see the broad curve of the dunes, deserted at this hour save for a flock of black-headed gulls, watching for fish on the incoming tide. The dim morning light gave an unearthly aspect to the landscape.

She was about to turn back from the window and return to bed when a sound from below made her stop in her tracks.

She froze momentarily and listened. There it was again, the sound of someone moving about downstairs. Taking her dressing gown off the back of the bedroom door, she picked up a heavy torch she kept by the side of her bed and crept onto the landing. Here she stopped, peering down into the lounge below her. In the semi-darkness she could make out the light of a small torch moving about. She began to make her way downstairs, careful to avoid creaking boards. At the bottom of the staircase she stopped. The light had suddenly

A Cromer Corpse

disappeared, but she knew that the intruder was still there in the room, for in the silence she could swear she could hear breathing. A cool gust of air informed her that whoever had entered the house had left the French windows open.

Panic seized her. She decided she must retreat to the bedroom and phone for the police. She turned quickly and almost ran up the first few steps, but she wasn't quick enough. She felt a sharp blow to the back of her skull, then blackness descended.

When she finally came to, she rolled over on her side, clutching her aching head. She looked at her hand. A crimson stain on her fingers. Staggering to her feet, she examined the scalp wound in a mirror. Fortunately it wasn't deep. Still groggy, she pulled a tissue from her pocket and, holding her head, looked about the lounge. It was now fully daylight and she was able to see the debris left by the path of the intruder.

The lounge was a mess. A chair had been overturned. Books and papers were strewn on the carpet, indicating that the intruder had systematically searched the room. Between the two bookcases stood a large escritoire. The front had been forced and the contents rummaged through. She examined the damage. Several savings bonds had been removed and two more of Monty's credit cards were missing. A small cash box which she used as a back up for the shop had also disappeared. She went to the drinks cabinet and poured herself a large brandy. Then she sat on the edge of the sofa and dialled for the emergency services, waves of shock overwhelming her. When she'd finished the call, she put down the phone and began to weep.

A Cromer Corpse
* * *

At precisely nine a.m. when Margaret Jones was dialling for the emergency services, Bottrell's mobile rang. Bottrell, who had just returned to Hautbois Lodge after a long walk along the dunes, answered it immediately.

"Charles here. Have you seen today's paper?"

"And good morning to you, Charles," Bottrell replied, unimpressed by his old friend's terseness. "To which particular paper are you referring?"

"Any damn paper."

Bottrell walked over to the front doormat and picked up his unread copy of The Mail. The headline read: NORFOLK BLACK MAGIC CASE. CHILD RITUAL MURDER LINK.

"I get the point, Charles," he replied, quickly scanning the contents of the article.

"Don't suppose you said anything to the media?" Grayling asked.

"You suspect right, Charles. It's not in my nature."

"No, I thought as much. Still, some bastard has leaked it. Possibly one of my team. I can do without this."

"I can imagine."

"Listen, John. I'm having a briefing at ten. Can you make it?"

"I'll be there."

"Good. Did you get to look at Druitt's correspondence, incidentally?"

"I did."

"And?"

"Nothing significant as yet. However, I got something altogether more interesting from his partner." Bottrell told him of the diaries. "One difficulty though."

"What?"

"The damn things are in a sort of code. Give me time and I may be able to break it."

A Cromer Corpse
* * *

By ten am the briefing room at Police HQ was even hotter than during Grayling's last meeting. Despite the appearance of three large office fans on floor three and the opening of windows, the room resembled a large sauna bath, the only difference being that the inhabitants of the room were entombed in uncomfortable suits and ties. Jackets had been thrown on the backs of office chairs and the customary tasteless coffee had been discarded in exchange for ice cold drinks.

Grayling himself, a traditionalist, stood suited in front of a large whiteboard. Beside him, looking slightly awkward, was Waverely, looking red-eyed and tousle haired. Bottrell, who was sitting in the front row, suspected a heavy night's drinking with the boss. But maybe not, considering the age gap. Nevertheless, he wondered. Grayling picked up a pointer stick and struck the whiteboard which displayed a series of photos and scribbled notes relating to the murdered girl.

"Okay, ladies and gentlemen, let's bring ourselves up to date," he began. "Annie Banham. We know from the forensic evidence she was drugged, then murdered, probably as part of some ritual at the midsummer solstice – June 21st – a year ago. She was last seen by her school friend, Susan Blight, at around 3.45pm on that day. We also know she'd arranged to meet her other friends, Abigail and John Stevenson at the concert the same evening at Blackling Hall but she didn't turn up. And her mother knew nothing about the arrangement. We've contacted the owners of the hall to see if we can re-examine the CCTV footage but so far this has yielded nothing.

A Cromer Corpse

"On the evening preceding her disappearance her father, Michael Banham, left the family home with the intention of moving to Scotland. Glasgow to be precise. We now know from the police there that he had a contact – a relative on his mother's side of the family. After staying in Dumfries briefly, he took up residence at a lodging house in the Gorbals area but subsequently disappeared. We know nothing of his movements prior to leaving for Scotland but it seems unlikely he intended to take his daughter with him. A month previously he had been involved in a fight in Norwich and we suspect he had mistreated his wife, although she didn't lodge a complaint against him.

"The two teenagers, John and Abigail Stevenson, were part of a pagan group in Norwich which Annie Banham attended on at least three occasions. We also know Montague Druitt attended some of these meetings. We have, therefore, (pointing to the board) " a direct link between Druitt and Annie. You will all of you be aware that the media have now cottoned on to this aspect of our investigation. I'm extremely angry about this. I don't know how the information was leaked but I do intend to find out."

Charles Grayling stared accusingly at his audience.

"What this means is that our procedure is made all that more difficult. There has also been a further development. Since two days ago there have been two burglaries, one at Druitt's bookshop, the other at his house. During the second break in Druitt's partner, Margaret Jones, was assaulted, though not seriously. Unfortunately she was not able to see her assailant. In both cases a quantity of cash and credit cards belonging to Druitt were taken. We've contacted the banks but unfortunately we were too late in preventing two large

A Cromer Corpse

cash withdrawals made in Norwich early this morning. It's possible that whoever did this also murdered Druitt. D.C. Waverely, you have something to add."

Grayling sat down, reluctantly removing his jacket as he did so. Waverley stood up, speaking to the assembly in a tentative but controlled manner.

"I've been accessing Druitt's computer and analysing his emails. He seems to have made contact with a wide variety of people on the net, some of them occultists, some of them freemasons. This, by the way, is in addition to the local contacts we already know quite a bit about. The list comprises individuals in the West Country and East Anglia but also further afield in Canada and the States, He was a member of an organisation calling itself "The Golden Dawn Revived", which originated in the States during the '50's. From initial information we have received from the FBI, it had a cult status. Its founder member, one Father Ignatio Paracelsus, aka John Piggott, served a lengthy prison sentence for child abduction during the early '60's and several other founder members also had criminal records. It also had a European chapter known as "The Sons Of Paracelsus" which has its headquarters in Amsterdam. Now we know that Druitt made several visits last year to Amsterdam to a man called Jan Van Verhoeven. Our link with Interpol in Holland tells us that Verhoeven is well known to them in connection with drug and people trafficking. Exactly what Druitt's connection with him is we're not exactly sure but we have a suspicion it may be drugs. That's as far as we've got."

Waverley sat down.

"Any questions?" asked Grayling.

A Cromer Corpse

Someone at the back of the room raised a hand. "You think it likely Druitt's murder is drug related?"

"It's quite possible. But that doesn't explain the peculiar circumstances of his death. The ritualistic nature of his killing would suggest another motive. We are assuming his killer had an accomplice. What we haven't been able to do is establish a clear motive. John, I believe you have something you want to say?"

Bottrell rose to his feet. "I've been doing some research into Druitt's background. Prior to his move to Norfolk, he'd established a reputation for himself as a leading pagan in West Country circles. For several years he rented premises near Wells where he organised courses in druidry, wicca and other aspects of paganism. His intention had been to set up a trust in memory of the late Gerald Gardner. However, he fell foul of the trustees and when the lease for the property ceased, he left in something of a hurry, owing the trustees money. One possibility is that someone followed him to Norfolk and took their revenge on him. It would explain the two burglaries. We know from Druitt's partner that he had been sent death threats and that the brakes of their car had been tampered with. Yesterday, following the burglary, I was given a set of journals belonging to Druitt which are in code. I'm attempting to break this code and when I do, it may bring us nearer to a solution as to the killer's identity. As for his connection with the death of Annie Banham, I'm not willing to speculate. According to John and Abigail Stevenson, he was interested in the notion of sacrifice, but in practice that could mean different things."

"Thanks John," said Grayling. "Current objectives then. DC Waverley and I will be interviewing Susan Blight, the friend of Annie Banham tomorrow. We are also waiting on SOCO's feedback on the two break- ins.

A Cromer Corpse
And DC Rankin will be travelling to Amsterdam to interview Van Verhoeven. Meanwhile, it will be business as usual with the house to house work. As regards the media, keep it stuum."

A Cromer Corpse

CHAPTER FOURTEEN

It was a small packet of white powder, measuring one inch by two. She had seen it on her mother's bedside table when she had walked into her room on the top floor of the big house. She had seen her mother tasting the white powder one summer evening when she had peered between the banisters at the people below. On that occasion there were at least fifty people in the great lounge, some dancing to music, some drinking and laughing, some kissing, others just lying on floor pillows, smoking from a large pipe which they passed around to each other.

She picked up the packet, opened it, then, licking her forefinger, dipped it inside and tasted the powder. It didn't have much taste she thought. She close the packet and went back into her bedroom. On the way she met her father. "I'm going for a walk in the wood," she informed him.
"Well, don't go too far. Breakfast is at nine, then we're going out for the day in the camper van." Her father smiled at her. That warm smile was something that she always remembered in latter years.
"I won't be long," she said. But, as it happened, she never turned up for breakfast. She was discovered wandering in the wood, her dress torn, her face scratched, unable to explain what had happened to her. Her parents never fully understood what had happened to her that hot summer's day. At first they thought she had been molested but she had no memory of an assailant. So terrifying had been her time in the wood she never had the courage to tell them all the details.

A Cromer Corpse

It had begun the moment she had entered the outer perimeter of the wood. As she stepped onto the path and the great beech trees above cut out the overhead sun, she had heard them. Voices whispering amid the trees. Ancient, cracked voices conspiring, mocking, threatening her. She had spun round, trying to trace the sound, but she had seen no one. The voices came and went on the breeze, now to the left of her, now to the right. Her pace had quickened and soon she had found herself stumbling along the path. But as she drove herself deeper into the wood, the trees around her had begun to change. Their barks took on the semblance of human flesh. Dark and wrinkled, some oozing blood, and when she dared to glance at them from the corner of her eye, she could see that they had eyes. Eyes that watched her every move.

She had broken into a sprint now, but still the voices had murmured and whispered and they were growing louder and more insistent. Then, as she came into a clearing, she saw the hut which Uncle had made the subject of their secret. Uncle was standing in the doorway of the hut, dressed in a black robe. He was smiling and exultant and when he saw her, his eyes glistened. Then her heart filled with horror for in his left hand was a long, curved dagger, the blade dripping with blood. He beckoned to her and when he began to laugh she knew that he had committed some unspeakable atrocity in that dark hut.

She screamed and fled back down the path whence she had come, but behind her she could his heavy tread, and his voice, urging her to stop. Either side of her the other voices whispered their dark conspiracies and everywhere there was the rank smell of putrefaction.

A Cromer Corpse

When she finally came to, she found herself lying on a patch of moss. Her dress was torn and there were scratches to her arms and legs. From far off in the wood she could hear someone calling her name. It was her father.

*   *   *

When Melanie arrived back home at lunch time she thought at first a fire had broken out. The lounge was shrouded in a dense haze of acrid tobacco smoke. In the centre of the floor, sitting cross-legged like a Buddha against a pile of cushions, sat John Bottrell, his favourite old briar attached to his nether lip, pipe bowl reeking. At his feet were countless pieces of paper. He was leaning over a black-bound book, his head in his hand. So absorbed was he in his task, he scarcely noticed her enter the room.

"Sorry," he apologised, looking up, "I was miles away."

"So I see. God, it stinks in here. I'm opening these French doors. I thought we'd agreed, John, pipe outside unless freezing weather."

"I forgot. I was absorbed."

"In the diaries. Any luck?"

"Absolutely zilch so far. I just can't figure this code out."

"Let's have a look," she said, peering at the book. She glanced at the heirogylphics displayed on the page:

"It's some sort of runic encryption as far as I can make out," Bottrell said, "but I just can't figure it out. I've been at it for three hours."

Melanie smiled and rubbed his hair affectionately.

"They're not runes, silly," she said, smiling.

"Well what are they? If you know, tell me, dammit!"

A Cromer Corpse

"It looks like semaphore. In fact I'll swear it is. I've seen something like it in a book I read as a kid. Hang on. I think I might still have the book."

She disappeared momentarily, then came back into the lounge holding a small paperback entitled "Secret Codes." Then she sat down on the floor beside him while Botttrell absentmindedly plugged the bowl of his pipe with fresh tobacco.

"Not in here," she demanded. He put the pipe aside. "Yes, as I thought. Look. Early semaphore."

He quickly translated the first few letters: "F-I-R-S-T D-I-A-R-Y E-N-T-R-Y."

"Still," she said, "you could be forgiven for thinking they could be a variant form of runes. Particularly the I and the N. Rather like the moon and yew runes in the Germanic system."

"I didn't know you knew so much about the runes."

"You might be surprised how much I know," she said, cryptically.

* * *

On a hot morning in late June, DC Rankin approached the tall, imposing police HQ in Amsterdam's Marnixstraat. Never having visited the city before, he was struck by its diversity and vigour and earlier that day had taken breakfast at one of the many street cafes which form a feature of city life. It was therefore with some regret that he pushed open the swing door of the large red brick building and was met with a blast of hot air from the stuffy interior.

Showing his warrant card to reception, he sat down on one of the faded hessian seats and waited as news of his arrival was conveyed upstairs. After a few minutes the lift doors opened, revealing a large plain clothes policeman with a head like an egg. Florid-faced, he had no eyebrows and Rankin noted his left ear lobe sported a gold stud. He smiled genially at his English counterpart, displaying a row of broken teeth.

"Detective Rankin? My name is Peter Groeller. Pleased to be meeting you. This way please."

The lift smelled of stale coffee and body odour. When they reached the fourth floor, Groeller punched out a security code beside a heavy brown door and the two men entered a large open plan room containing about fifty officers, some seated at computers, others answering phones or standing chatting in their shirt sleeves. They approached a tall, grey-suited man with cropped blonde hair, white at the temples, who Groeller introduced as his DCI. He shook Rankin's hand and smiled.

"Our friend Van Verhoeven is in interrogation room three," he advised him. "My officers woke him early so he isn't well pleased with us. So far he's being co-operative but I can't predict it will last long." He indicated Rankin to sit down. "A bit of background before we start the questioning."

"By all means," replied Rankin.

"You got the bare facts I faxed?"

Rankin nodded. "That he's a nightclub owner and his premises he uses as a front for drugs."

"Quite so. However, what my fax didn't include was the information about his ownership of several fishing vessels. About a week ago one of these vessels was found by customs to have a quantity of heroin on board. It was immediately impounded and the skipper arrested. Van Verhoeven himself claimed to know nothing of the cargo. And so far the crew are saying nothing. Since they were registered as self employed he's been able to cover his tracks, claims he had no knowledge of the drugs of course."

"You mentioned he had no criminal record?"

"That's true – which makes our job more difficult. He always works through intermediaries it seems. He's like a spider, sitting at the centre of its web. He knows precisely what's going on, feels the tremors but he himself is never accountable. His name often crops up obliquely, through third parties. And he's smug. The room's here. On the left."

Groeller opened a door and they entered a small, windowless room lit by one neon strip. Van Verhoeven was leaning back in one of the black plastic chairs, hands clasped behind his head. He was grinning as if he were enjoying some private joke. On the table in front of him was a small black ash tray and in it burned a long Havana cigar. He looked at his wristwatch.

"You've been keeping me waiting, gentlemen. I hope this will not take long. Time is money."

Rankin noted he spoke with an impeccable English accent, his Dutch origins betrayed only by the occasional vowel. "This is the English officer you told me about? This must be very important for him to have travelled so far to meet me. It's my pleasure, sir."

He extended a tanned hand in greeting. Rankin declined the offer and the three detectives sat opposite him. "You don't object if I smoke?" He sucked at his cigar, emitting a long stream of smoke in their direction.

"Let's get to business, Van Verhoeven," said Groeller. "I must remind you you are not here under caution."

"Just helping with enquiries. Just so. So what do you want to ask me about?"

"About the death of Montague Druitt."

"Ah, Mr Druitt."

"An associate of yours?" asked Rankin.

A Cromer Corpse

"Mr Druitt and I enjoyed a few business dealings, yes. I was sorry to hear of his demise."

"The day before he died he told his partner he intended visiting you at your offices here in Amsterdam. Apparently he never made it. What was the nature of his intended visit?"

"Mr Druitt and I share an interest in incunabulae."

"In what?"

"In rare books and manuscripts. Mainly of an occult nature. I collect such items. We came to know each other a few years ago through a chance meeting on the internet. I had a particularly rare copy of the Malleus Maleficarum which he was interested in purchasing. I was offering it at a very reasonable price. Far cheaper than the price it would have commanded at auction for example."

Rankin leaned forward. "What do you know about an organisation calling itself "The Golden Dawn Revived"?"

Van Verhoeven smiled, tapping his cigar into the ash tray. "An American organisation. I have heard of it."

"Are you a member?"

"No I am not."

"And the 'Sons Of Paracelsus'. Are you a member of that organisation?"

"A European occult group."

"Whose headquarters is here in Amsterdam."

"So I believe. Yes, I know of this group."

"Are you a member of it?"

"No, though I know several individuals who are."

"And how do you know that?"

"Because they are customers of mine through the book trade."

"Were you aware that Montague Druitt was a member of The Golden Dawn Revived?"

"No, I was not aware of that."

A Cromer Corpse

"Strange that in his numerous visits to you the subject never cropped up in conversation then?"

"Not at all strange. Our conversations were purely of a business nature. We rarely discussed personal matters."

"And apart from selling Druitt rare books you had no other business dealings with him?"

"None at all."

"Which seems odd, doesn't it, considering the large sums of money which appear in Druitt's account, monies deposited from a Dutch account on a regular basis. On July 15th, for example, a sum of three thousand pounds. What was that for?"

"A rather fine collection of books I recall, including a John Dee and a copy of "Liber De Angelis" –a very rare volume."

Groeller sighed. It was clear Van Verhoeven would reveal nothing more to them. Van Verhoeven looked at his watch.

"Is there anything else you wish to ask me about, gentlemen? If not, I have a busy day ahead." He stood up as if to leave.

"You are free to leave, Mr Van Verhoeven. However, we may wish to ask you further questions."

"Very well. Then I shall say au revoir for the present. It has been a pleasure to make your acquaintance, Mr Rankin." He held out a brown, jewelled hand again but Rankin turned away from the triumphant smile and opened the interview room door. A waft of eau de cologne passed him as the blonde Dutchman left.

A Cromer Corpse

CHAPTER FIFTEEN

At 10 am on July 5th, the emergency services received a call from Hautbois Hall.

"My name is Bradley Evans. I think I've murdered someone," the voice said.

When police arrived at the Hall fifteen minutes later, they found Evans standing outside the main door to the property. He was clutching a kitchen knife and his t-shirt was splattered with blood. He pointed in the direction of the Hall, saying: "He's through there. In the kitchen."

Alex Smith was found lying on the kitchen floor by police officers. He had sustained three stab wounds, one to his left arm, one to his left cheek and a much deeper wound to the thorax. His eyes were closed but he was still breathing. The medics who arrived minutes later administered immediate first aid and he was rushed to the Norwich Hospital A&E.

When Charles Grayling interviewed Evans at 11.15am later that morning, the latter was still wearing his shorts and trainers, though the t-shirt had been removed pending possible forensic tests. Alex Smith was given immediate surgery for the most serious of his wounds and placed in the intensive care unit.

In Interview Room 15 at Police HQ, Grayling sat with Rankin, facing a pale-faced Evans. He was an unlikely figure for a potential murderer, Rankin thought. His tear-stained face and shaking hands indicated that this attack had been motivated by extreme passion rather than cold-blooded calculation. With his balding head,

A Cromer Corpse

large doe-like eyes and flabby, tattooed arms, he cut a comical figure.

"Is he dead?" Evans asked.
"Fortunately for you he still lives, though he's sustained serious wounds."
"You'll be charging me with attempted murder then?"

"At the moment we're not charging you with anything. We wish to talk to you."
"I want a solicitor."
"You can have one later when we conduct a formal interview. Now we just talk to you."
He started to sob.
"I didn't intend killing him. You must believe me. We'd had a terrible row. He was taunting me. Told me I was past it, that I was a failure. I couldn't stand it, couldn't bear it. I picked up the knife. He was pushing me, so I lashed out. Next thing I knew he was on the floor. I thought he was dead." He stopped. He was trying to catch his breath and was shaking uncontrollably.

Grayling leaned forwards. "Calm down," he said. Have a cigarette."

Rankin opened a packet, lit a cigarette and passed it to Evans. There was a silence. Then Grayling continued.
"What was the row about?"
"Monty."
"You knew he'd had an affair with Monty?"
"I suspected he'd been unfaithful."
"And you suspected Druitt?"
"I feared it was him, yes. About a week before Monty disappeared I followed Alex. He said he was going to Norwich to the health club but he didn't. He went round to the Lodge and stayed there for two hours."
"You challenged him?"
"I said nothing at the time. I saw him coming out with Monty though. I wish I had."

A Cromer Corpse

"Tell me about your relationship with Druitt."

"We were friends."

"Come on, we know it was more than friendship."

Evans stared back at them. "Alex told you that?"

"We know you and Druitt had been lovers. We also know you were on close terms with him when he lived in Somerset, that you had business dealings when he lived there. Explain that to me."

He sighed. "Alex never knew the full extent of my relationship with Monty. It happened before I met him of course. We met when he visited Wells and gave a talk there on the life of Gerald Gardner. At that time he had the big house in Somerset and was trying to promote the trust."

"The Gerald Gardner Foundation."

"You know about that?"

"Go on."

"I was a member of a small group – a wiccan group. This was before I became interested in freemasonry. Anyway, we met at a pub in Wells shortly afterwards. We were immediately attracted to each other. Not just in the physical sense. There was something about Monty, a spiritual dimension. A lot of people noticed that. He was one of those ascended souls."

"Can we stick to the facts?"

Evans recoiled at the blunt intervention.

"Very well. Monty set up the trust about a month after we met. By that time I was seeing him on a fairly regular basis. He had a meeting at the big house – Sandford House it used to be called then. He'd managed to enlist the support of a number of influential pagans. Most pagans I've met over the years don't have a great deal of money, you understand, so what he'd done was quite impressive."

"Who were these people? Can you give us names?" asked Rankin.

A Cromer Corpse

"There were two university professors. I never knew their real names. They were incognito because of their academic positions but one of them I recognised because of his media reputation: Professor Wilkins of Oxford University. He was an historian. There were two Americans. Businessmen. Oh and a Dutchman, also a businessman. He never said much."

"The Dutchman," Grayling interrupted. "Describe him."

"Blonde, short, middle aged. He smoked large cigars and wore some jewellery."

Grayling looked at Rankin. "You don't recall the name?"

"Van something. I don't remember exactly."

"Continue."

"Monty had plans. The hall was going to be turned into a pagan conference and festival centre, an international setting for pagan events. But he also planned to turn some of the rooms into offices. There was to be a magazine and a media officer, that sort of thing. And part of the house was to be a museum with a permanent collection of pagan artefacts, a research facility and also a library. He'd planned it all."

"And the funding – where was that to come from?"

"Fund raising among pagan groups initially, in the West Country, though the bulk of the investment would be from the committee members."

"And you lent Druitt money?"

"Yes."

"How much?"

"Six thousand."

"Which wasn't repaid."

"That's right. The scheme never came to fruition. Monty lost the lease on the house and he had debts. Bad debts. None of us knew that till afterwards."

"How did that make you feel?"

"What do you mean?"

A Cromer Corpse

"Did it make you feel vengeful?"

"What are you implying?"

"Surely you were resentful. £6,000 is a lot. You must have harboured feelings of resent."

"It wasn't like that."

"Oh, what was it like?"

"Monty made it up to me. He gave me three oil paintings he'd acquired – as recompense. They were worth a deal of money."

"So you got your investment back?"

"Not entirely."

"And when you found out your partner was having an affair with Monty, you felt angry?"

"Yes, I was angry."

"I get the feeling you're not being entirely straight with me. I think you knew about the affair for quite a while. Some weeks before Druitt disappeared in fact. Isn't that so?"

"Certainly not."

"You've not been entirely honest with us. You'd started to follow Alex and you'd found out about their meetings at the Lodge. So you decided you'd kill him. Isn't that really the truth?"

Evans' face had turned red and Rankin noted he was sweating.

"That's rubbish," he said, his voice rising.

"So you planned to kill him. You arranged to meet him on the pretext of some business arrangement. You drugged him, put him in his car, drove it down to the dunes, murdered him. Then you got someone to help you shift him onto a fishing vessel, mutilated the body and dumped him at sea, hoping no one would ever find him. Isn't that the truth?"

Grayling was staring fixedly at Evans as he uttered the accusation. There was a long pause. Then Evans said quietly: "I wish to see a solicitor."

A Cromer Corpse

* * *

Melanie had seen it straight away but he hadn't. That annoyed him. He'd always been good at cryptograms and codes. Or at least he thought he had. But there it was, staring him in the face, and he hadn't even thought of semaphore. It wasn't easy to read of course. The symbols had been committed to the pages often in a great hurry so that at times they were indistinct or resembled each other, especially the symbols F and R. Transcription was therefore slow and laborious.

When Melanie left for work at the end of her lunch hour he seated himself on a pile of cushions in the lounge with the diaries on his lap and a reporter's pad within easy reach. Then he plugged his pipe with a rich mixture of aromatic and Dutch shag tobacco and, lighting a match, drew it back and forth over the charred bowl, watching as the sweet smelling smoke curled into the air. He had determined he would air the lounge thoroughly before Melanie returned at 5.30pm so that she wouldn't have cause to complain. When he'd lived on his own in the years following Frances' death, there hadn't been a problem with his pipe smoking. For days on end he'd sit in his flat, plunged into the profoundest melancholia, smoking pipe after pipe until the small lounge resembled a Victorian opium den. There were no visitors then for he encouraged no one to call, despite the occasional well meaning phone call from colleagues or distant relatives. He would sit, lost in reverie, absorbed in memories of happier times.

As he picked up the first of the black journals he thought of Frances and the old pain came flooding back. The memory of that last night and the meal with her parents in Kent was as vivid as if it were only yesterday. The

A Cromer Corpse

dark night and the journey back via countless winding country roads were engraved on his brain and the shadow of that fateful night had never entirely left him. He had caused her death, through his state of being and his inattention at the wheel. He alone had killed her and he would never forgive himself for that.

He drew on his pipe, opened the book, then began transcribing. The entries were in date order, the first going back six years and the early accounts related to the big house in Somerset and the organisation of the pagan festivals there. This was all pretty routine stuff. However, there were a number of rather cryptic references to sums of money, followed by the initials "VV." This was surely the Dutch businessman Grayling had mentioned to him on the phone. Clearly Druitt had had dealings with this man way back. Were these legitimate transactions? Probably not. Several other people and groups were mentioned: a pagan group called "The Children Of Artemis", another entitled "The Sons Of Paracelsus." Frustratingly they were only mentioned in passing. There was also mention of something called "The Archangel Ritual" but again no specific details. It was all very tantalising. After an hour of this he lay down his pipe and made a coffee which he laced with a large measure of malt whisky.

When he returned to the lounge and settled down again he found the combination of the coffee, alcohol and lack of fresh air had made him drowsy. He lay back on the cushions, the pipe still attached to his lip and closed his eyes. Within a few minutes he was asleep. He was dreaming now, dreaming of Frances. He was behind the wheel of the car, driving along a narrow road. Dark trees loomed either side. Frances was next to him, her head back, slumbering. As the road wound to the left, then right, he found himself losing concentration. Then he seemed to lose consciousness. Minutes later he woke. In

A Cromer Corpse

the pitch dark he could make out Frances next to him, her eyes closed, her flesh white as chalk. He raised his left arm, touched her face, but it was cold. Then he saw the great crimson splash of blood on her nostrils and mouth. There was something else too, a smell of burning plastic.

He glanced in the rear view mirror. The back of the car was on fire. He struggled to release Frances' seat belt but his had been somehow locked by the impact. It was no use. He couldn't even reach his phone. The smell of burning was getting stronger, acrid fumes now filling the interior. There was an explosion and a great sheet of flame burst from the back of the car, engulfing them both. He cried out, gasping for air. He could see his jacket on fire, feel the heat burning his flesh. *Not here. Not trapped here inside this steel coffin.* He pulled with all his strength at the locked belt, cursing. And all the while the stench of burning plastic grew stronger and the pain seared into his arms and torso...

A Cromer Corpse

CHAPTER SIXTEEN

Monkhampton was a small town which lay on the north west coast of North Norfolk, some six miles from Cromer. In its heyday in the Edwardian period, this thriving seaside town had earned the title of "The Jewel of East Anglia", being served by Brunel's Great Eastern Railway line, but since then it had fallen gradually into decline. Although it retained many fine residential villas and elaborate shop fronts, it struggled to retain its identity. Many of the grand houses had become residential nursing homes or downmarket B and B's while the former fishing fleet had been reduced to a handful of crabbers which produced slim pickings for the hotel trade.

It was just off the main street in Monkhampton where Grayling and DC Waverley found No 27 Cromer Road, residence of the Blight family. Since it was a Saturday and they had arrived early, Grayling had parked the car near the front and strolled purposefully along the promenade, followed closely by his much younger colleague.

"Shabby genteel is the phrase for it, Waverley," he pronounced as they seated themselves outside one of the small promenade cafes with their cappuchinos. For Grayling, it was a liquid breakfast. He rarely looked after his stomach properly, bombarding it with alcohol and fried food.

"The phrase for what sir?" Waverley asked, obtusely.
"This town. Like me, it's seen better days."

A Cromer Corpse

Waverley found herself agreeing. She looked at Grayling's worn face and portly figure but said nothing more.

"So. Susan Blight. Remind me of what we have, will you?"

Waverley opened her folder. "According to John and Abigail Stevenson –"

"The Goths," he interrupted.

"Yes sir, the Goths. According to them, Susan Blight was supposed to have arranged to meet Annie Banham on the evening of the 21st of July at Blackling Hall. They didn't say whether the two girls were to arrive there together. Susan Blight last saw Annie at 3.45pm that same day."

"When school concluded?"

"Yes sir. That's it. According to the Stevensons, she and Annie dabbled in witchcraft. Annie also attended some of the Norwich moots, as, presumably, did her friend Susan."

"Was she interviewed shortly after Annie's disappearance?"

"Only briefly, as were several of her class mates. Nothing significant to report."

Grayling looked down at the beach where two elderly residents were picking litter from the foreshore. It was going to be another hot day he thought.

"Anything else?"

"No, nothing more."

He finished his coffee and stood up, reluctant to leave.

"Right, let's get to it then."

* * *

Bottrell woke with a start, the memory of the dream still fresh in his mind. For a moment, the awful picture of the

A Cromer Corpse

burning car and Frances' inert body next to him overwhelmed him. He bent forward on the cushion, clutching his head, sending the diaries spilling onto the floor. That's not how it was. Yes, he had crashed the car and woken to find his wife lying dead next to him, but there had been no fire and he had escaped alive. This was not his dream. Surely he had tuned into something else, someone else's horror.

He stood up, swaying slightly from the effects of the alcohol induced sleep and opened the French window, letting in a draft of cool air. This was not a unique situation, he reflected. Many times in the past he had been able to utilise the "psychic gift" as his mother had always described it. He had no control over what happened to him but he knew that often the events he witnessed in these dreams had some basis in reality. He walked out onto the patio and stood for a while, smoking his pipe, the cool breeze stroking his face. Then he went inside and looked at his watch. He still had another two hours before Mel returned from the bookshop. He must resume the transcription of the diaries. First, though, a short walk down to the dunes. He needed to connect.

* * *

May Blight was a tall, attractive woman in her early thirties, expensively dressed and with a tan which suggested frequent trips abroad. She sat opposite Grayling and Waverley, holding a china tea cup in her hand. Grayling noted the smooth, manicured fingernails and whitened, regular teeth. Beside her sat Susan Blight, a virtual copy of her mother with the same, sleek blonde hair and slim build. But unlike the mother, Grayling detected a precociousness about the daughter. He

A Cromer Corpse

gripped the small china cup in his large hand, downing the tea in one go, then reached for his cigarette packet, but thought better of it.

"How can we help, Chief Inspector?" asked Mrs Blight. The voice was contained, the consonants clipped, but there was a faint hint of estuary English.

"We'd like to ask Susan here a few questions about Annie Banham," replied DC Waverley.

"She was my best friend. I miss her," said Susan.

"I'm sure you do."

"Have you found out who murdered her yet?" She was sitting on the edge of the sofa, hands clasped, knees together. Her eyes were wide and she looked like a rabbit startled by car headlights.

"Not yet Susan. That's partly why we've come to see you. You were with her on the day she disappeared, weren't you? You'd arranged to go to a concert together on the evening of June 21st. Is that right?"

Mrs Blight squeezed her daughter's hand but she withdrew it from her grasp.

"Susan had arranged to go without my permission," said Mrs Blight. "I was rather upset about it. She told me she was going up the road to do homework with a friend."

"We'd really like to hear Susan's account of what happened," observed Grayling.

"But she already gave police a statement last year."

"That may well be so but now the enquiry has reopened we need to re-examine the evidence."

"We'd arranged to meet at Blackling Hall around 6.30pm. There was a tribute band playing – Black Sabbat. We'd been told about it by John and Abi."

"The Stevensons?"

Susan nodded. "That's right. There's a fence which is on the east side near the woods. You could get in easily then but they've since repaired it. We were going to

A Cromer Corpse

meet up there. Lots of people from school knew about it."

"And the last you saw of Annie was when you left her at the end of school?" asked Grayling.

"Not exactly. We walked to her house. When we got there her mum was in a state. He dad had upped and left that afternoon. He'd said he wasn't coming back. But he'd left a letter for Annie."

"What did the letter say?"

"She wouldn't tell me, but she seemed upset about it. I asked her if she was still coming to the gig. I thought, maybe – you know. Anyway she said she would."

"Did she mention anything about meeting anyone else in the interim?"

"No one."

"Did she say anything about her father to you?"

"Only that she wasn't surprised he'd done that. She said he used to knock her mum around when he got drunk. She'd told me before about it."

"And when you left her, how did she seem?" asked Waverley.

"Upset of course. Well, she would be, wouldn't she?"

"Then what happened?"

"Then I went home, had a meal and left around ten to six, just as we'd planned. I got to the wood around half six I guess and hung around for ages but she didn't show."

"Where you met the Stevensons?" asked Grayling.

"That's right."

"Tell me more about John and Abi."

"What do you want to know?"

"They were pagans, weren't they?"

"They're Goths. And pagans."

"And you and Annie had quite a bit in common with them. That's right isn't it?"

"Annie did more than me. She was into witchcraft, spells, that sort of thing."

A Cromer Corpse

"And were you into witchcraft too?" asked Waverley.

Susan shrugged. "I was interested, yes." She glanced at her mother who was looking distinctly uneasy.

"Annie and me used to go into her mum's garden shed and do stuff."

"What kind of stuff?" asked Waverley.

"Healing spells, that sort of magic. Annie was very worried about the planet and what was happening to it. We did spells together to help the animals and sick people. She had a book she kept the spells in. We'd light incense in there and say the spells together. That's all."

"And there were just the two of you? No one else?"

"Did you ever attend meetings in Norwich with John and Abi?" interrupted Grayling.

"Sometimes, yes. They gave us a lift in."

"You told me they were Earth Mysteries talks," said Mrs Blight, frowning.

"I told you that because you wouldn't have approved. Mum's a Christian."

"I understand, Susan," answered Grayling. "Now I want you to look at this photo. Tell me, did you ever see this man at one of the Norwich meetings or any other meetings you and Annie went to, perhaps when you were with John and Abi?"

Susan peered at the photo of Druitt.

"Yes, I recognise him. His photo was in the papers, wasn't it? He's the man they found in the sea off Cromer."

"That's right. But did you ever meet him?" Grayling persisted.

"He did come to a couple of the meetings. He gave a talk. It was about the history of witchcraft."

"And were you and Annie introduced to him?"

"Not exactly. Annie and me were with John at the time. He talked to John quite a bit. He asked us our names, too."

A Cromer Corpse

"Did you or Annie see him at any time after that? Did he ask you to his house, for example?"

"Not me, though I saw him with Annie and John once."

"When was this?"

Susan scratched her head.

"I'm not sure exactly. Let me think…I bumped into them one weekend in Morton. They were coming out of a café. They didn't see me at first. They were busy talking. It was the summer, a few weeks before Annie disappeared."

"Early June?"

"I guess it was."

"And at that time did Annie ever mention this man to you?"

"No. She used to talk about John and Abi a lot. By then we weren't on quite such good terms."

"You were still doing your magic together?" asked Waverley.

"Not so much by then. Annie used to meet up with John and Abi at weekends to do some ritual. She never said much about it. Something to do with the old gods she said. They'd take Annie off to places in the countryside and do open air stuff. One time she asked me if I'd like to come along but I said I wasn't really interested. After that I got the feeling she'd lost interest in me, so I didn't ask her much about what she did. Why do you keep asking questions about this man ? Had he something to do with Annie's death?"

"We're just exploring possibilities at the moment," Waverley explained.

"I always thought he was weird."

"What do you mean?"

Susan looked slightly embarrassed.

"Well, I caught him looking at Annie on one occasion. You know, pervy."

"Why didn't you tell me?" asked Mrs Blight.

A Cromer Corpse

"It didn't seem that important. Besides, I don't tell you everything."

"And did he ever look at you in that way?" asked Waverley.

"No, not really. What I meant is he was staring at her like you would if you stared at a picture in an art gallery. Know what I mean?"

"As if Annie was an object?"

"That's it. Like she was in a museum or something. I found it creepy. I still have some of Annie's stuff upstairs if you're interested."

"What things?" asked Grayling.

"Old photos of me and her. And the diary we kept when we were doing magic. I meant to give it back to her but I never did. She wrote most of the stuff anyway."

Her eyes filled with tears and Waverley offered a reassuring hand.

"You must be very upset about losing your friend."

"They were very close," observed Mrs Blight. "Is that all, Chief Inspector?"

"That's all. Oh, and if we could take a look at Annie's possessions – and the diary?"

"I'll take Susan upstairs and get them for you."

When they had left the house, Grayling sat in the car and examined the contents of the plastic folder Mrs Blight had given him.

"Some bits of driftwood, a pack of Tarot cards, photos – could be of some use – and here we are, the diary. We'll take a closer look back at HQ," said Grayling.

"You were right, guv, about the connection between Annie, Druitt and the Stevenson twins," observed Waverley. "Do you think the girl told us everything?"

"I thought she did. Remarkably forthright for a teenager. What's now obvious is that the Stevensons haven't given us the complete picture."

"You'll be interviewing them again then?"

A Cromer Corpse

"You bet."

A Cromer Corpse

CHAPTER SEVENTEEN

Bottrell recharged his pipe for the third time, lit it, then opened the journal. The first volume was a strange compendium of memoranda, cryptic entries regarding financial transactions and philosophical musings, mainly concerned with magic and freemasonry. The dates in this first book belonged to the period prior to Druitt's move to Norfolk and there were several references to "The Trust", including the names of individual benefactors, including Bradley Evans and a "VV" – a reference, no doubt, to Van Verhoeven.

As he laboriously translated the cryptic figures, he became increasingly frustrated by the lack of personal detail contained in the journal. There was a complete absence of any reference to Druitt's wife, for example, and no mention made of his relationship with Evans. The tone of the journal was cerebral and philosophical. Occasionally, Druitt would refer to something he called "The Great Work," a cryptic phrase which he failed to elaborate on. The phrase rang a chord in the back of Bottrell's brain. Where had he come across that phrase before? In the works of Aleister Crowley? Or was it John Dee, the Elizabethan mystic? He couldn't be sure. There were also references to Johannes Cunalis, the author of the medieval grimoire he had found among Druitt's possessions. He resolved to find out more about this priest from Munich.

Druitt appeared to be ambivalent about Gerald Gardner. Sometimes he commented favourably, whilst at other times he was scathing, accusing him of pedantry and myopia. His comments on freemasonry were perhaps the most curious of all. As far as Bottrell knew, most freemasons were inclined towards Christianity and certainly believed in a benign creator. Druitt appeared ambivalent. "A mason," he wrote, " is obliged by his treasure, to obey the moral law. He will therefore never be a stupid atheist or an irreligious libertine. He, of all men, must understand that God sees not as man sees, for man looks at outward appearances but God looks to the heart. Let a man's religion or mode of worship be what it may, he is not excluded from the Order, provided he believes in the glorious architect of heaven and earth. What name we give to that Architect does not matter: Baal, God, Lucifer. They are but different names for the great primal life force which is in all of us. Tap that life force, be a part of it and we shall achieve a kind of immortality. What matters is the path we make to that connection. When the spirit is exalted, the power will be unleashed."

Bottrell paused and re-read the passage carefully. The means rather than the end. The ambivalence of the Creator. Is that what Druitt was driving at? And what exactly did he mean by that last phrase? Sure, he understood the concept that the Creator had many faces. But how could Druitt reconcile Satan and God? But then a thought occurred to him. He had come across this principle before in his reading of the ritual magic of Eliphas Levi. Like the alchemist, the magician uses the divinity of his choosing to exalt his own spirit and achieve some sort of spiritual ecstasy or union with the Divine Will. Maybe that's what Druitt was driving at? But if that was the case, then he still didn't understand fully the connection with freemasonry.

  He turned the page and decoded another entry, this time in red ink. The passage read: "Gnothi Seauton: Know Thyself, Control Thyself, Make Thyself Noble and Therefore Divine. Forget not the three pillars of the

A Cromer Corpse

Temple: Wisdom: the intellectual power which directs the work: Strength: the moral force which executes it and Beauty: which constitutes the harmony of the intellectual power, the consonance between design and deed. The Master of Freemasonry attains, in the final enlightenment, deep knowledge and power over life and death. Remember this!!"

There followed several, even more obscure entries which Bottrell could make no sense of. Was Druitt simply delusional or was he a magician who had acquired real power? And if the latter, whence did that power derive?

He heard a sound at the front door and looked up at the clock. It was later than he thought. Melanie was back. It occurred to him that the room was now full of tobacco smoke. Too late to rectify the situation. He closed the book then reluctantly extinguished his pipe.

* * *

The following day was even hotter. By 9am every window in police HQ at Norwich had been opened wide but since there was no movement of air and the air conditioning was faulty, the rooms remained hot and stifling. DC Rankin arrive at a quarter past the hour, proudly driving the new Chevrolet he had purchased the previous day. It was, he told other officers, his way of dealing with the effects of global warming. Rankin had spent his formative years in Inverness where the weather had been distinctly cold even in summer, but that was more than a decade ago. For the past three years he had worked for the Norfolk constabulary where he had become used to a series of summer droughts. As he entered the lobby, his jacket slung over his shoulder, the duty sergeant called out to him.

A Cromer Corpse

"DC Rankin? Message from DCI Grayling. You're to report to his office immediately, sir."

Rankin glanced at his mobile but there was no text message which might have indicated the summons. But then Grayling didn't really believe much in technology, he remembered. Still, what else would you expect from a man in his '50's who'd spent his formative years working in the Met in the 70's? In those far off days, he reflected, it was all Ford Granadas, car radios and back handers which oiled the Force. DNA and computers hadn't yet been discovered.

"Thanks, Smithy," he replied. "What sort of mood was he in when you last saw him?"

"The usual."

This was Smithy's shorthand reply for acerbic. He had hoped for "as cheerful as the old bugger can be" or something similar but he remained disappointed.

Since the lift was still out of order, he climbed the stairs. The air was like an oven interior and there was a smell of stale bodies. At the top of the flight he met DC Waverley.

"Grayling's waiting to see you. There's been a breakthrough."

"On the Druitt case?"

"On the two burglaries."

The swing doors to floor three opened. Grayling stood there, shirt open, forehead perspiring, stomach bulging over his trouser belt.

"Rankin. My office please."

He followed Grayling into his office where a table top fan whirred at high speed.

"SOCO have given us a matching thumb and forefinger print regarding the burglaries. One in Druitt's bookshop, the other in his house. And we have a name."

"Yes?"

A Cromer Corpse

"One Peter Riscorla. Local fisherman. Lives in Morton. And he was known to Druitt. Has a record too. GBH - a pub fight in Cromer two years back. A couple of other minor offences, one juvenile, breaking and entering. Ring any bells?"

"None."

"Well, he's our man, anyway. Lives in one of those fishermen's cottages near the front in Morton. I suggest you two go and pick him up for questioning. I shall be here, trying to sort out the Banham case. Bottrell phoned this morning. He's starting to build a profile on Druitt. Says there may well be a link with Annie Banham. The two knew each other after all. And we shall need to re-interview the Stevenson twins. I thought this pm or tomorrow. The mother works in the day and she'll need to be present."

"Any progress in the diaries regarding Van Verhoeven?"

"Not so far. The diaries are in code, so progress is slow. Anything from the Dutch police yet?"

"Turns out Van Verhoeven was one of the founder members of the "Sons Of Paracelsus", though he denied it when I interviewed him. We're in contact with the FBI who are sending us a file on the organisation, including a list of its prominent members. Should prove useful."

"Keep me posted. Curse this damn heat!"

* * *

Holman Terrace was a row of Georgian cottages close to the esplanade in Morton. At the end of the terrace stood Morton Antiques, but today the blinds were down and the closed sign hung behind the front door. Peter

A Cromer Corpse

Riscorla lived at number three, a two up, two down, which had seen better days.

Rankin rang the bell, then stepped back onto the pavement and waited alongside DC Waverley. After a brief pause a window above them opened. A woman in her mid forties leant out, arms folded over ample breasts. Rankin noted her arms were tattooed and she had the face of a Romany woman. Her jet black hair was pulled back into a bun and from her ear lobes hung two silver earrings shaped as crescent moons.

"Yes. What do you want?"

"Not what but who. We want to speak to Peter Riscorla. Is he in?"

The window slammed shut, then there was a long pause before the front door opened. Close up the woman's face seemed coarser thought Rankin. She was wearing a pair of tight denim shorts and a short t shirt which failed to conceal her bulging midriff. She smelt of cheap perfume. Rankin showed his warrant card.

"DC Rankin. This is DC Waverley."

"What's this about?"

"Peter Riscorla. We want to speak to him urgently."

"He didn't come home last night. He's probably on the boat. Could still be at sea for the morning catch. Is this about the murder?"

"It's not about the murder. Does he have a mobile you can reach him on?"

The woman turned and walked back into the hallway, returning with a phone.

"He's switched it off."

"What's the name of the boat?"

"The Endeavour. Dark blue with a yellow stripe along the stern."

They found the Endeavour, moored by the harbour wall. There was no sign of life at this hour save for a solitary

A Cromer Corpse

fisherman, standing smoking his pipe at the end of the pier. He turned to stare at them.

"Looking for someone?"

"Peter Riscorla."

The fisherman strolled towards them, a short, squat man with a strong Norfolk accent.

"Saw him late last night in the Running Hare. Usually his boat's still out at this hour. Must still be on board. Missed the tide. Maybe sleeping it off."

Rankin and Waverley stepped on board, Rankin calling Riscorla's name. There was no reply. They descended the narrow steps to the small cabin. Even before Rankin entered, he could smell the blood, the sickly sweet smell turning his stomach. He opened the cabin door and his worst suspicions were confirmed.

A man's body lay sprawled across the small bed, his head thrown back at an incongruous angle, his left arm half concealing a swarthy face. Across his throat was a deep gash and gouts of blood stained the pillow and sheets a deep crimson. Judging by the amount of blood, Rankin reckoned the jugular had been severed. Because of the angle of the head, the eyes of the victim appeared to be staring straight at the two police officers, an effect which they found deeply unnerving.

Rankin moved forward, careful not to contaminate the crime scene. He leaned over the body and, donning a surgical glove, touched the forehead of the victim.

"Must have happened several hours ago," he said. He examined the room. There were clear signs of a fierce struggle. Broken crockery lay on the floor along with an upturned whisky bottle whose contents could be smelt in the fetid air of the room. An ash tray had also been overturned and there was a smell of charred carpet.

Rankin looked at the body of Peter Riscorla again. There were gashes on the outstretched hand where he had tried to ward off his attacker but there were also

A Cromer Corpse

other wounds: burn marks on the forehead and chest. On the floor by the bed was a large leather briefcase which had been upturned, its contents strewn across the floor.

Waverley knelt down and began poking at the papers with the end of a biro. Bills, bank statements and a day to day diary caught her eye. Rankin glanced down at what she was doing as he took out his mobile and began punching in the HQ number.

"Better leave it all to SOCO," he advised her.

She nodded. The two officers closed the cabin door and made their way back up on deck. The man on the pier paused over his pipe to wave at them.

"Found him?"

"Yes thanks, we found him," Rankin called back.

A Cromer Corpse

CHAPTER EIGHTEEN

It was the tall man with greying hair who told her her parents were both dead. She had lain in the bed for two days, face swathed, not daring to ask. But when she did enquire, the nurse asked her to wait and the tall man in the dark suit entered her room and sat down on the edge of her bed and explained what had happened to them.

She had tried to weep, but her face had contorted with pain so that she cried out in anguish, the doctor holding her undamaged left hand, trying to comfort her. When he had left the room, she had lain back on the pillow, the pain ebbing and flowing through her face, trying to imagine how they had died in that blazing inferno, knowing she would never see them again. And she had thought of Uncle. Where was he? Had he too died in the blaze?

When the nurse returned, she asked her about him. The nurse said he would visit her for sure. It was only a matter of time. But as the days came and went and the hot days of July gave way to the cooler days of August and then September, still Uncle did not come. No one came to comfort her except the doctors and nurses. As time passed, her mind went back over the events, and she tried to make sense of it all.

She remembered how noisy they had all been in the car, especially her mother, and how Uncle had driven the car at high speed along narrow country lanes, and she recalled clinging on to her seat as they plunged into the darkness ahead. There had been some sort of

A Cromer Corpse

animated discussion, she couldn't recall what it was about. The next thing she knew was the collision and the car turned upside down, her mother's face covered in blood, the blank eyes staring at her, head twisted towards her from the front seat. Uncle's distraught face as he pulled at the crushed door, trying to get her father out. But it was no use. Her father's lifeless torso lay across her, trapping her. And then the explosion, and after that, the darkness, engulfing her. Where was Uncle? Why wasn't he in the hospital? What had become of him?

At the end of the first week, she had the first operation. It was to be one of many operations, each one more difficult and more painful than the last. Then followed the long days when she lay in the stuffy hospital room with only the medical staff as her visitors, the pain like an inferno in her face, her only comfort the sounds of birds outside in the hospital garden and the shafts of sunlight which fell across the bottom of her bed in the early mornings, then travelled across the floor and illumined the wall opposite by early evening. Small comforts these, but they gave her sustenance.

Some eight weeks later, after the fourth operation on her face, they took away the bandages and brought her a mirror. She stared at the wrecked face before her, deep, livid scars running across her forehead and cheeks. It was like looking at the face of a stranger. Then loss and disconnection overwhelmed her. At that moment she knew that her life would never be the same. Her old existence was lost without trace. She would never see her parents again.

It was in the second week after the last operation that great Aunt Mary came to see her. She had only a vague recollection of the little grey-haired woman in the tweed

A Cromer Corpse

suit who sat opposite her in the day room. But she had a kind face and her eyes twinkled when she spoke. She explained to her that since she was her only living relative, she would be coming to live with her in a small cottage on the edge of the sea in Suffolk.

She had never been to the east with her parents. She finally arrived on a cold, windswept day in mid September. She got out of the car and stood on the headland, staring out at the broad, flat bay, ringed with dunes. She was struck by the immensity of the sky. The grey, flecked ocean stretched out towards the north and east and the cold wind cut at her face. To her young and impressionable mind the place seemed eerie and menacing.

"What's that?" she asked, pointing to a ruined building on a low hill in the distance.
"A medieval priory – well, the remains of one," Aunt Mary replied. "There was a great church here once but many centuries ago the sea flooded the land and it slipped into the sea. This cliff edge used to be the graveyard. Sometimes, at low tide, you can see bones sticking out from the edge of the cliff. Bones of the old monks, I expect."

At first she thought she would not take to Danewych with its deserted beaches and low, windswept hills. But as the weeks passed, she found herself becoming attached to the place. It was a ravaged, inundated landscape where, for centuries, different peoples had struggled for supremacy. She also had been ravaged, her face half burnt away, then reconstituted. She had been torn from her parents and cast alone into an unfamiliar world. Great Aunt Mary was kind and considerate to her. Despite her advanced years, she found time to take

A Cromer Corpse

her for long walks along the deserted beaches and she came to learn the names of many birds.

As winter moved slowly into spring, she saw the seals basking off Mariner's Point and watched in wonder as the brent geese swept in over the land to their nesting places. Occasionally they would take the bus trip together into town and breakfast in the old tea rooms. But always she was conscious of her face and of people staring at her. She felt easiest when she was alone with her great aunt, never much enjoying these excursions.

From the moment she stepped into the Old Acre, the small, two bedroomed cottage where her great aunt had lived alone for twenty years, she had been fascinated. It was like travelling back in time. The lounge was the largest of the rooms, equipped with a large open fireplace and a battered sofa and chairs. It reeked of age. From the overhead beams hung a series of corn dollies, some fashioned as figures, others elaborate horns of plenty. And at one end was a small witch figure, exquisitely dressed, riding a broomstick.

"What's with the witch?" she had asked Great Aunt Mary.

"I bought her in a French market in Stowmarket years ago," came the reply. "She has been my close friend and confidante over the years. Together we do magic."

The phrase intrigued her. What exactly did she mean? Over the next few weeks she was to find out.

Aunt Mary, it transpired, was what might have been termed in another age, a wise woman. Her kitchen was crammed full of bottles containing tinctures from plants and trees, designed to cure every conceivable malady. "My learning, such as it is, doesn't come from books," she told her. "My mother taught me everything, how to heal and how to curse, how to make spells, how to look

A Cromer Corpse

into the crystal ball and see into the future. People these days scoff at such things but I know they are true because they work. Call me a witch if you like. I don't give a stuff what people think of me. Take these warts on your hand for example. I'll soon get rid of them!"

And get rid of them she did. She took a piece of raw beef, rubbed them, then buried the meat in the garden. Within two days the warts had gone. It was that moment which marked her initiation into the cunning arts.

* * *

Bradley Evans was just putting the closed sign to open when he noticed Grayling ringing the doorbell next door. For a moment panic seized him. Then he realised with relief that he was not the object of their enquiry. He had spent most of the previous night by Alex's bedside at the Norwich Hospital and had been relieved not only at the progress he'd made but also the fact that Alex had decided not to press charges against him.

The door to number three Holman Terrace opened and the swarthy woman with ample breasts appeared, cigarette in hand. Evans had seen her before behind the bar in The Leaping Hare, flirting with customers, an activity not offered to Evans and Smith. He had thought the woman coarse and ugly.

Grayling and Waverley sat in the small lounge while the woman finished her cigarette. She looked shocked at the news she had just received.
"Wendy. Wendy Evans," she was saying to Grayling.
"And your relationship to the deceased?"

A Cromer Corpse

"Girl friend. But I don't understand. I was with him last night."

"Where exactly?"

"In The Hare."

"And afterwards?"

"I left around 11.30pm. Roger – that's the landlord – operates a lock in with some of the regulars. Peter usually stays on drinking with his mates. When he didn't come back I thought he'd go straight to The Endeavour."

"When you left the pub, who was he with?"

"No one in particular. He was chatting with Roger I think."

"Tell me, do you recall him having an argument with anyone yesterday?"

"No one. Peter knew a lot of people locally of course. He was well know in Morton and at Cromer, especially among the fishermen."

Did he have any visitors recently?"

"Now you mention it, yes he did. I came back yesterday afternoon and there were two men in suits waiting on the doorstep. I thought they were Jehovah's Witnesses so I told them to get lost. One of them, the older of the two, got quite nasty. They kept asking where Pete was. I told them he was on the boat."

"You told Peter about this?"

"Yes. He didn't say anything. Just looked thoughtful."

"Describe them."

"The older one was short and stocky. Blonde hair. A foreign accent."

"What sort of accent?"

"Not sure. Could be German. Oh, and he had an earring."

"And the other man?"

"Also short. Dark haired. Big build. He didn't say much. They looked like bouncers. I didn't like the look of them. You think they may have had something to do with Pete's death?"

A Cromer Corpse

"Maybe. Do you know this man?" Grayling showed her a photo of Druitt.

"That's Monty. I knew him. We both knew him. He was a friend of Pete's. Used to drink with him in the Hare."

"How well did you know him?"

"Not that well. As I said, he was Pete's friend."

"Did he come here often?"

"He was often here, yes. He and Pete had some sort of business arrangement. Pete never told me what it was. Something to do with importing fine art. Sometimes they went off in the boat together. They had a link with somebody in Holland."

"Wendy, we shall need to search the house."

"Why?"

"We have reason to believe Peter was responsible for two recent burglaries in Morton."

"News to me."

"I don't doubt it. We shall also need to fingerprint you. You'll need to come down to the station. DC Waverley will take you."

"Do you have a search warrant?"

"Do we need one?"

She shrugged resignedly. "It's all the same to me if you have or haven't."

When Waverley had left, Grayling began searching the premises. He started with the lounge where he examined a small writing bureau. It wasn't locked. Inside were a number of unpaid bills, a passport, driving licence and a large day to day diary and pocket address book. The two latter items he placed inside an evidence bag. He quickly scanned the kitchen, then made his way upstairs. There were two bedrooms, the larger of which contained a water bed and several items of female clothing strewn across the counterpane. On a side table stood a framed photo showing Peter Riscorla standing arm in arm with

A Cromer Corpse

two other men. One, a short squat individual with cropped hair, he did not recognise. The other was Montague Druitt. Opening the back of the frame, Grayling took out the photo and placed it inside his coat pocket. Then he went into the second bedroom.

This room was barely furnished. It contained a single bed, a computer and a long bookcase, most of whose shelves were filled with assorted papers, ornaments and a few books. He scanned the shelves. One volume caught his attention. It was an old book with faded gold lettering, whose spine read: "The History And Traditions of Freemasonry." He took it down and opened it. The flyleaf bore the inscription: "From Monty to Peter: With Fond Regards, Summer 2006. Congratulations on your investiture."

He put the book to one side, then leafed through the remainder of the shelves. The last volume turned out to be a small photo album containing a number of shots of Riscorla with Wendy. There were also photos of a harbour but it was not anywhere on the East Anglian coastline, he was sure. Then, on the last page, he found it: the first clue in an otherwise baffling business. It was a photo of three men sitting drinking at a bar. Behind them, on a wall, was poster bearing a Dutch inscription. One of the men was Riscorla, the second was Druitt and the third, he was certain, was Van Verhoeven.

A Cromer Corpse

CHAPTER NINETEEN

Grayling had just packed the PC and the evidence bags into the back of his car when he thought he might carry out one final reconnoitre of 3 Holman Terrace. It was something he often did at scenes of crimes. It was like turning a painting upside down. You often viewed it with a fresh perspective.

He finished his cigarette, sat ruminating for a while behind the wheel, then went back inside. The house was silent save for the cries of gulls echoing in the distance, He began going through each room, trying to build up a picture of the couple who had lived here. Theirs had been a casual relationship, he was pretty sure of that. The discarded bottles of wine and whisky, the waterbed and the general air of chaos in the cottage indicated a lifestyle that was far from cosy and domestic. But what he hadn't discovered so far were the items removed from Druitt's home and bookshop. If he was a close friend, why had he burgled Druitt? And what exactly had he been looking for? Incriminating evidence perhaps? And what, he wondered, was Van Verhoeven's part in all this?

He walked into the second bedroom but found nothing new to interest him. He went over to the window and pulled up the blind. The summer sunshine flooded in, blinding him momentarily with its intensity. He found himself looking down into a concrete yard at the back of the house, which was vacant except for a dustbin and a small red micra. He went downstairs and, finding the back door to the kitchen unlocked, passed into the yard.

A Cromer Corpse

The micra was an old model, F reg., the red paintwork faded and there was a large dent in the driver's door. Kneeling down, he began to examine the tyres. Two new remoulds at the back but the two at the front were badly worn and had a number of flat spots on the inside edges. He recalled the tyre marks found near the beach where Druitt's car had been discovered. Could this be the murderer's vehicle? He took out his mobile and began dialling the vehicle registration centre.

* * *

Bottrell was walking along the dunes when his phone rang and he received the news of Riscorla's death. Grayling explained the circumstances in his usual, matter of fact way.

"Any progress with the Druitt diaries yet?"

Bottrell stared out to sea. It was a sunny day and the sun glistened on a calm ocean, giving it the appearance of a polished mirror.

"Slow but steady. Druitt was a complex character it seems. Well, when it came to magic, anyway. There's also a strong link between the magic and the freemasonry. Anyway, I need to discuss this properly with you. Can we meet?"

"I'm up to my eyes at present. How about this evening in the Hare?"

"About eight?"

"I'll see you there. Oh, one other thing. I've got the FBI file on the Sons of Paracelsus. Do you have a fax machine?"

"I don't but the bookshop does." Bottrell gave him the number. "I'll take a look at it. How's that suit?"

"Fine by me. Around 3pm?"

A Cromer Corpse
"It's a deal. And how about a drink later on? At the Leaping Hare?"
"Consider it a date."

* * *

It was half day closing in Morton. Melanie, who had spent the morning minding the Aerial bookshop, put up the CLOSED sign when Grayling arrived and he and Bottrell retired to the room at the back which usually served as the office. Equipped with sandwiches from the local Spar shop, they sat down and Grayling reached for the FBI file.

"It appears that The Sons of Paracelsus was a cult organisation, founded in Philadelphia in 1958 by a Roman Catholic Priest, one Father Ignator Paracelsus, alias John Piggot," said Grayling.

"I've heard of it."

"Piggott drew his inspiration from two sources:," Grayling continued. "The magical writings of Aleister Crowley, whom he met in Hastings in the late 1940's. Secondly, two magical grimoires or books of spells known as the *Liber de nigromancia* and *Das puch aller verpoten kunst* (The Book of All Forbidden Arts) by Joahnnes Hartlieb (1400 – 1468). Not much is known about the authors of these respective books. Hartlieb served the Duke of Bavaria in Munich during the last three decades of his life."

"And the other one, Joannes Cunalis, author of *De Nigromanica*, was a Munich priest, birth date unknown. All that I know is that he was a cleric in minor orders and that his work came to the attention of the archbishop, who destroyed the book. Fortunately he had made another copy."

A Cromer Corpse

"Right. Which was later printed in 1585 in Berlin. It is this edition which Piggott appears to have acquired," said Grayling. "Now this is where it gets interesting. In the early 1950's Piggott made a trip to the Isle of Man and visited the Museum of Witchcraft in Castletown, which was then run by Gerald Gardner, the occultist. Gardner and Piggott had struck up an acquaintance and they continued to correspond for some years afterwards. Finding Piggott's brand of necromancy too extreme, Gardner ended the relationship some time in the mid '50's. In 1958 Piggott, then a serving Catholic priest, founded The Sons of Paracelsus. Within two years he had established links for his organisation in at least three European countries, including the UK, France and Holland. Some of his members were former OTO adherents, others freemasons. A rare pamphlet, printed privately by Piggott in 1961, sets out the principles of the organisation. You've read this document I take it?"

"I haven't. The fax machine went haywire at page ten and I lost the rest of the file."

Grayling passed over his copy of the FBI file. Bottrell scanned it.

We draw our inspiration from the writings of Paracelsus and his "Alphabet of the Magi", but also the great magical treatises of the middle ages. Like Paracelsus, we believe that the self may be transformed through magical ritual, the carving of talismans and the practice of astrology. We believe Magic is the holy fountain where faded beauty finds once more its adoration and where obscured wisdom regains its light. Magic is the inspiration for all life, uniting Man with the Cosmos. It destroys the barriers which the Prejudices of Science and Reason have set up between Man and Man: it withdraws the golden robe that decks the soulless body. It brings heart to heart and strength to strength. As in

A Cromer Corpse

the noble art of freemasonry, so in Magic we strive through the use of symbolical forms to work for the Greater Good, seeking to ennoble ourselves and others in order to bring about a universal Brotherhood of Humanity which we aim to represent in miniature among ourselves. Thus the Sons of Paracelsus shall be a beacon to humankind.

"It seems Piggott believed that the "ennobling of the magician's soul" could be best achieved through contact with what he described as "angelic presences", these often being mistaken by Christian theologians for demons," continued Grayling.

"That's familiar to me."

"In order to achieve this, a circle would be drawn: a quadruple band with a pentacle inscribed in its centre, with a sword depicted at the top, extending down across all four bands, with its point on the top of the pentacle and other figures or markings on the upper left, lower right and lower left. The cardinal directions were then given outside the outermost band, with east on top. Within the bands the names of 16 spirits were inscribed."

"Pretty standard stuff in occult terms," said Bottrell.

"The magician would then conjure the spirits and command them to carry out his will in the name of God," Grayling continued. "Piggott stresses that the concept of God is entirely pantheistic. He equates the word with that of "life force" or "divine inspiration." One of the most important aspects of the magical operation he defines as "the willing sacrifice." By this he means the physical death of a creature or person who, by rendering up their soul, heightens the spiritual energy of the angelic presences and of the operator. "Sacrifice," he comments, "is an age old principle, not only of pagan belief but of the Hebraic system. We have only to look at the story of Abraham and Isaac to understand this profound truth. By sacrifice the magician unites his own self with that of the cosmos."

"I note that bit about the physical death or a person or creature."

"Indeed. He also believed in the power of visions and in the use of crystals to achieve this. Like Cunalis, he thought that the art of scrying was best achieved through the use of a child, *for their vision is undimmed and pure by nature. The virginal nature of a child cannot be matched. A child is the pure vessel through which spiritual clarity and mastery can be achieved.*"

"OK. What else have we got?"

"In 1963 Piggott was found guilty in the Philadelphia State Court of the abduction of a twelve year old girl, one May Bridges. Piggott had lured the girl to the house he was then renting and had kept her prisoner for a period of two months. There was no evidence that he had molested the girl during her captivity but the prosecution did provide evidence that he had included her in a number of rituals, one which necessitated her being tied hand and foot to a large wooden pentacle in the cellar. He was sentenced to ten years' imprisonment in the Philadelphia State Penitentiary but was subsequently released on the grounds of ill health. On his release he travelled first to France where he met followers of the Order, then to Holland where he was instrumental in setting up a new Chapter of the Order."

"Anything else?"

"At present there is a total of twelve Chapters in Europe and America and two in Canada. The UK Chapter was established in 2004 by Montague Druitt and two other members."

"He's still alive I take it?"

"Piggott died in 1995 under mysterious circumstances. His body was found in an Amsterdam canal in December 1995. Cause of death: drowning. And his abandoned bicycle was found nearby. It was not clear whether he had been pushed into the canal. When his apartment was searched a great number of papers and books were examined by the Dutch police. His computer subsequently revealed links with a number of known paedophiles."

When Grayling closed the file, Bottrell sat thinking. He said at last: "Do you think Druitt murdered the girl?"

"I think it's possible. Especially after reading this. Though not from a sexual motive. What I don't get is the link between freemasonry and magic. I always thought freemasons were Christians."

"In theory, yes. Well, they believe in God, anyhow. They refer to Him as the Architect of The Universe. Clearly Monty was reinterpreting masonry to fit his own brand of necromancy. He wouldn't be the first magician to do that. Aleister Crowley followed the same esoteric route and upset a number of masons as a result. The problem at present is there's no direct evidence linking Druitt to Annie's murder. Then there's the question of what happened to her father."

"Listed as a missing person?"

"Yes, and he disappeared the same day Annie went missing. He's still a suspect. What we do know is Druitt and the fisherman, Peter Riscorla, were both masons as are Alex Smith and Bradley Evans. And the Dutch businessman, Van Verhoeven, had links with the Paracelsus cult. There's a web emerging, but I'll be damned if I can find out who's at the centre of it."

Just then the phone rang. Bottrell picked it up.

"It's for you."

"Grayling here. Right. OK."

" They've just found Riscorla's car. And they checked the tyre treads. They match the prints left at the Druitt murder scene."

A Cromer Corpse

CHAPTER TWENTY

That evening The Leaping Hare was heaving. It was Friday night. In the public bar the local darts team were competing against the Cromer contingent and the tables were full of large men supping real ale.

Bottrell found Grayling in the Smoke Room at the back of the pub. He was wearing a crumpled grey suit and lounging back in a faded leather armchair. Next to him, perched awkwardly on a tall bar stool, sat DC Waverley, looking slightly uncomfortable.

"Glad you could make it," said Grayling. "Mine's a malt. Hannah here will have a coke, thanks. She's detoxing – and driving."

Bottrell soon returned bearing the three glasses. Over nearly thirty years of their acquaintanceship, Grayling's self destructive drinking habits had not changed. But then Bottrell himself was well accustomed to the solace that hard drink offered the mind. After Frances had died, he had descended into a maelstrom of unremitting alcoholism, ignoring the advice of well meaning friends and colleagues. It was partly this which had speeded his departure from the Met. There was, after all, much comfort to be had from the blurring of reality. Much like his pipe, the golden amber liquid was for him a balm.

"So you got a match?" he asked Grayling.

"An exact match. There's no doubt Riscorla was responsible for Druitt's death. What we now need to know is the wearer of the small trainers."

Bottrell searched his memory. "Ah yes – the print also found by the car."

A Cromer Corpse

"Riscorla took a size 10. Rankin checked."

"What about his woman?"

"The girlfriend? Not the right size. No, he had an accomplice but we don't know who."

"Helen Druitt?"

"A possibility, yes. There were those threatening letters."

"So who killed Riscorla then?"

"Search me. Waverley here spent some time in the pub here at lunchtime. Came up with something interesting."

"Landlord recalls two men in the pub the day before Riscorla disappeared," said Waverley. "Said they sounded foreign. Possibly east European – but not Estonians. He knew that because the cleaner at the pub is Estonian. They were asking for Riscorla."

"He gave a description?"

She smiled. Bottrell thought it was a coy, rather attractive smile. He felt a certain sympathy for Waverley, stuck with this old curmudgeon. "A detailed one. They spent half an hour in here, then left. Another thing. Riscorla's girlfriend said she was visited by two men later the same day. One had short blonde hair and a foreign accent. Had an earring. The other was dark."

"You think Van Verhoeven sent them?"

"Quite possibly. By the way, we've had the car examined. We found traces of heroin in the boot. We're also searching the boat," said Grayling.

"You think he was murdered because of drugs?"

"There's a triangle here: Riscorla, Van Verhoeven and Druitt. They were importing drugs from Amsterdam and now two of them are dead. Question is who killed them. Did Van Verhoeven's men kill Riscorla? And why did Riscorla kill Druitt and ransack his place? Who was his accomplice? Talking of Druitt, what progress with those diaries?"

Bottrell filled in the background regarding the grimoires.

A Cromer Corpse

"You read the FBI file? What did you make of it?"

"I'm convinced Druitt abducted and killed Annie Banham, though I don't know how. Druitt had this idea of the power of the virginal child as a spiritual channel. It's there in the diaries but it's even more manifest in Piggott's pronouncements. You know he died in Amsterdam?"

"Yes. His death was unexplained. I read that."

"Wonder if there's a link?"

Grayling drained his glass.

"Maybe. Let's have one for the road."

* * *

That summer was one of the hottest on record. For some weeks in the July of that year she seemed to slip into a dream world. She ate little, dreamt much and spent her days relaxing on the broad, flat sands of Danewych. Great Aunt Mary, who had a job as the manager of a charity shop in Stowmarket, did not comment on this extended period of idleness. She knew that she must leave her to get on with the business of healing herself. When the two met at their evening meal, she would merely enquire: "Had a good day?" and she would do nothing more than smile at her in response.

The beach at Danewych became an oasis of tranquillity. Where she chose to lie and sunbathe few tourists intruded save for the occasional dog walker and, from her chosen spot, a long dune, she could see far out to sea where the flat line of the empty horizon gave her solace. Here nothing disturbed her save for the melancholy cry of the gulls and the sound of the wind, shifting sand. She used to lie back on the sand, looking up at the huge sky, wondering what it might have been like here five

A Cromer Corpse

hundred years ago when there was a community and a thriving priory. Now all was lost beneath the waves.

One afternoon as she lay dozing, she thought she could hear the tolling of a distant bell, but she soon realised it was nothing but a fantasy. Images of the big house in Somerset crowded in on her. The dark wood, Uncle's face, the evening of the long drive, her mother's bloodied, pale face and the silence of that night. No matter how long she lay on the beach, she could not shut out the images. When she opened her eyes and glimpsed the sun above her, she was back in the wrecked car again with the smell of smouldering upholstery and metal and when the wind blew across the dunes, she was once more by the roadside, the cold biting at her charred face and arms, crying into the silence.

As July slipped into August, she felt the wind from the east turn in her direction. Her place in the dunes became colder now and she was forced to walk along the sea shore to keep herself warm. She found herself utterly alone as she walked northwards, past the sad ruin of the old priory, the edge of the land merging with the misty sky line. At times the roar of the waves seemed to absorb her very being and the past was forgotten, freeing her from her torment. A solitary figure on the immense beach, she was as one forgotten, a piece of flotsam cast up here by the immensity of the ocean.

One day she set off for the beach early, determined to swim round the headland to the other side where there was a small private beach, not overlooked by houses and inaccessible to walkers. A cold wind blew but the weather was set fair and the sky was cloudless. She plunged into the waves and began to swim out, using strong, even strokes. She found the currents stronger than she had anticipated and soon realised that she was making little progress. Then the sky began to darken and she was aware of a large cloud mass moving towards her

A Cromer Corpse

from the east. She began to tire now, each stroke taking more effort than the last. The beach which was her destination seemed further off than ever. She decided to turn back but no sooner had she done so than she felt a strong rip tide clutching at her legs.

She went under then, pulled down beneath the cold waves like a piece of jetsam. She kept her mouth shut and struggled, pushing her way back upwards. At last she broke the surface, gasping for breath, her energy almost spent with the effort. Then the rain began, lashing her face, beating at her head. At that moment she was overwhelmed by the sudden desire to relinquish herself and the thought of an eternal rest began to steal over her. If she gave way now, the past would be extinguished instantly and the wearisome business of existence would slip away from her.

She stopped struggling and allowed herself to float on the surface of the waves, closing her eyes. The last thing she recalled was an arm closing around her neck.

When she finally came to she was lying on her back on the beach with a man's jacket wrapped round her. A face peered down at her. Dark eyes and bleached blonde hair. He looked like a surfer.

"You almost drowned," he said. "Didn't you know about the riptide at Hellesdon Point?"

The surfer's name was Michael. He was strong, muscular and softly spoken. From the moment she opened her eyes she knew that there was between them an inextricable bond, a fascination. The affair that followed lasted two years during which time she thought of nothing else but Michael. He became, in a real sense, her reason for living. He lived in a small chalet about a mile from Hellesdon Point and here it was the couple met and made love with a regularity and intensity which she had only dreamed was possible. That someone would could love her and worship her in the way that

A Cromer Corpse

Michael did she found utterly inexplicable. But love her he did.

She never forgot the hours they spent together in the chalet, laughing, reading, making meals, locked in each others' arms. For her, Michael was also an anodyne. She was able to block out the awful memory of her parents' death and the man who had caused it to happen. The beach and the hut became her inner sanctum, the fulcrum of her new life.

Then, quite suddenly, after eighteen months of happiness, her world collapsed. In the September of that year, Michael began to complain of feeling tired. At first she thought he had picked up a virus from the surfing but when he did not properly recover, tests revealed he was in the grip of lymphatic cancer. He was given six moths to live by the consultant.

On the day they returned from the hospital, she sat in the chalet with Michael, watching through the window as waves crashed on the beach. It was a high tide and the sky was black with storm clouds. In that moment despair filled her and she knew that in some way she had been cursed. First her parents. And now this. All whom she loved were snatched away from her. Her mind drifted back to the cabin in the woods and its occupant. What dark magic had he wrought there and what influence had it had upon her life? It was as if he had woven a cloak and placed it about her shoulders, cutting her off from those she dearly loved. She swore then that if she ever met him again she would be avenged for the harm he had caused her and the suffering she had endured.

Michael fought like a tiger against the cancer. He submitted to radio and chemotherapy. He suffered sickness and his hair fell out. Still he rallied and, even until close to the end, insisted on swimming with her.

A Cromer Corpse

The chalet by the edge of the sea became their refuge from the world. Here they would sit for hours, listening to music together, talking about the past, hearing the sound of the sea. And all the while she was thinking of Uncle and the house and the cabin in the woods and the night of the crash and the long weeks of operations and recovery.

Great Aunt Mary gave her all the support she could muster. She prescribed herbal remedies for Michael and practised simple healing rituals for him. She was grateful for this but knew in her heart that in the end it would change nothing.

One day, among Aunt Mary's large collection of books, she found a volume of witchcraft traditions. In it was a section on magical rituals which would harm enemies. On one page was a picture showing a sheep's heart, stuck with pins. It was then she formed the idea of how she would work the destruction of Uncle and by stealth and cunning bring about his inevitable downfall. She copied out several spells and slipped the piece of paper into her journal.

Michael died in the hospice in the November of that year. She sat by his bedside with Michael's parents, watching him slip into a morphine-induced coma. He died just before 6pm. As he passed away, the skies outside the hospital darkened to the colour of pitch and swathes of rain beat down on the roof of the building. She sat peering out through the rain-spattered window, a terrible pain engulfing her. She had lost her soul mate, her reason for living. Never again would she feel his caress or hear his voice. Although Michael's parents showed her kindness, nothing would remove the pain of his loss, In her distress, she took to walking the foreshore. She trekked for miles, collecting small pieces of driftwood and pebbles as she went. On such expeditions she spoke to no one.

A Cromer Corpse

Not even Aunt Mary could get through to her, so profound was the misery she felt. She began to fill the chalet with the detritus she had collected from her forays along the beach. Wood and stone began to collect on tables and when the tables were full she began to hang things from the walls, so that in time the chalet became a living shrine to Michael's memory, a constant reminder of the time they had spent together. Then, one evening in February, there was a large storm which accompanied a high tide. When she went down to the chalet she found to her dismay that the sea had breached its entrance, taking with it much of her precious collection. She saw this as a message from the otherworld. Michael had gone forever now and she needed at last to move on.

A Cromer Corpse

CHAPTER TWENTY ONE

When he got back from the pub, Bottrell undressed and slipped quietly into bed. Melanie, who was still awake, turned and slid her arm round him. He nestled into her soft body and soon they were making love.

For some while afterwards he lay awake, listening to the distant sounds of the waves crashing on the beach. A ray of pale moonlight fell on the counterpane of the bed, giving a silvery glow to the room. He tried to sleep, to turn his thoughts away from the subject of Annie Banham, but he found himself recalling another time, some thirty years ago, when he was serving in the Met.

He had been working with Grayling on a paedophile ring which had international links. A team of three officers had been given a tip off and gone to a house in Bexley, Kent. It had been a hot day and he'd remembered the neat, four bedroomed houses with their well manicured lawns, long driveways and double garages. Their suspect was a GP, freemason and local philanthropist. When they'd questioned the man, he'd seemed eminently reasonable. A short, squat individual with a rounded face and beaming smile, he'd denied all knowledge of the names they'd presented to him as contacts. And the house was clean. No pornographic material, nothing which might fit the profile. They had left the house and were sitting in the car when suddenly Grayling spoke.

"The cellar," he'd said. "The house has a cellar."
Bottrell had sat looking at the GP as Grayling and the accompanying officer had broken the lock on the cellar door. He had turned the colour of chalk and was

A Cromer Corpse

sweating profusely. When they finally got the door open and turned the light on, they could hardly believe it. The room, which was padded, was kitted out like a TV studio, while the walls were equipped with an array of chains and instruments of torture. But the images which he could never get out of his head and which haunted him ever afterwards were the faces of the three young girls who sat cowering in the corner. They said nothing, fearing their persecutors, staring at them, their innocence stripped away under the harsh neon lights, their childhood irrevocably tainted.

They brought them upstairs and called for assistance while Bottrell handcuffed the doctor, charged him and escorted him to the squad car. He sat in the back of the vehicle while Bottrell watched him in the rear view mirror. The smooth, rounded face bore no sign of remorse, just apprehension. He wished he could put his hands round that plump neck and squeeze the life from him but he knew it was impossible and that it would bring him no pleasure.

He slipped out of bed and made his way quietly to the kitchen where he sat smoking for a while and staring out into the moonlit night. Far off, in the bay, he could make out a pool of silver light and hear the slow crash of waves on the deserted beach.
He finished his pipe and wandered into the lounge where he found Druitt's diaries and his copy of the *Liber di Nigromancia*. He began leafing through it, stopping half way to examine this entry:

"To find out about a theft, take a virgin girl of legitimate birth, at an hour before noon, and scrape well the thumb nail of her left hand with a knife. Then bind the thumb, beneath the nail, a slip with the following names on it: Benoham, Heresim, Medirini, Aliberri and Halba. If the

A Cromer Corpse

girl sees something, bind a strap of sheepskin on the slip round the thumb while saying this conjuration: "O you demons who have appeared before me in the nail of this girl, I order and conjure you that you shall have no power to withdraw with your companions until you have fulfilled my will. And if you disdain to do this, I command that you be bound beneath the waters of the sea by these names: Joth and Nabnoth, by which Solomon bound demons in a glass vessel. When you have said this, if the girl does not speak straightaway, recite this conjuration in her ear: 'I conjure you, virginal youth, by the true God Basyou, to have no power of concealing from me, but to manifest all that you see.' When you have spoken this conjuration three times, the girl will see all things clearly."

There followed further rituals and conjurations accompanied by a scribbled note in Druitt's hand which read: "Try henbane – gets better results."

Bottrell finished his pipe and closed the book, thinking of the cellar and the three girls they had found captive there. Druitt was not a paedophile. They'd found no evidence that he was. Yet in some way his intentions had been darker. How long had he used Annie Banham as a channel for his dark arts? And why and how had he disposed of her? What had been his purpose? He sat in the armchair and tried to collect his thoughts but all he could think of was how much he missed Frances. His mind began to meander and suddenly he was back in time, walking along a stretch of Cornish cliff they had once shared together. So vivid was the memory he began to weep.

The lounge door opened. Melanie stood there, hair tousled, eyes full of sleep.
"Come back to bed," she said.

A Cromer Corpse

*   *   *

As Bradley Evans entered Ward 21B, a smell of bleach and floor cleaner met his nostrils. He walked slowly along the ward, observing the patients: an old man with yellow flesh, masked by a nebuliser, a large black woman surrounded by smiling relatives; a thin, young girl with long black hair and an awkward smile whose face was the colour of chalk. He found Alex at the end of the ward, lying back on the pillows, an ipod clamped to his head. For a moment he stared at Alex's fine, high cheekbones and long eye lashes, wondering how it had come to this. He opened his eyes and removed the ipod.

"Didn't you bring anything for me? Grapes for instance?"

The voice was hard and sardonic.

"I'm sorry. I forgot."

"Then why the hell have you come?"

Evans grabbed a chair and placed it beside the bed.

"Alex, we need to talk. There are things we need to discuss."

"I've got nothing to say to you, Bradley."

"Look, I know what I did was - unforgivable." He struggled to say the word for, secretly, he had forgiven himself.

"But there are things we must talk about."

"What are you talking about?"

Alex gripped the bed sheet. His voice was cold and resolute. "There is no us, Bradley. When I get out of here I shall be seeing the solicitor. I want out of the business."

"You don't mean that."

A Cromer Corpse

"I mean it. Haven't you got somewhere to go? A shop to run?" He turned his face to the pillow. There was a long silence.

"The police came to see me, Alex."

"So?"

"Not just about you and me. They asked me about Monty. I told them you were having an affair. I think they suspect me."

Alex stared back at him. "And why shouldn't they suspect you?"

"What are you saying?"

"That evening before the Lodge meeting, when you went to Norwich to see about that Jacobean mirror."

"What about it?"

"You came back late. Or don't you remember? And without the mirror."

"I told you. Stephens had already sold it to a dealer. I told you that. Then I met Harry in the Forum. We went for a drink."

"You expect me to believe that crap? I lied for you Bradley. I told the police you were with me that evening. What were you really doing? Did you arrange to meet Riscorla? Was that it? Maybe I should tell the police the truth."

Evans stood up. "This is madness. You're not yourself. I can't talk to you when you're like this."

Alex gestured with his hand. "Go away Bradley. Go back to the shop. I need to sleep."

* * *

For some hours after he had returned to bed Bottrell lay awake thinking about Annie Banham's death, listening to Melanie breathing, feeling the warmth of her body beside his. Then at long last he drifted into sleep.

A Cromer Corpse

When he awoke he found Mel had already left for work. He glanced at his watch. 10am. He washed and shaved, then went downstairs to make some breakfast. On the table was a note which said: "Didn't like to wake you. Meet in the Hare 1pm for a drink? Love, M."

He had just poured the milk on his muesli when his mobile rang.
"Mel?"
"Is that John Bottrell?"
He recognised the voice. The thick burr was unmistakeable. "Dave Thomas. Good God."
"Got it in one. How are you?" It was thirty years since they had spoken. Dave Thomas had worked with him on the Bristol murder case which had been one of his first major West Country assignments. "Still with the Avon and Somerset?"
"Certainly am. And it's Chief Inspector Thomas by the way."
"I'm impressed."
"So you should be. Listen John. A hack called Goodman gave me your details. It's in connection with this Druitt case. Who's heading the investigation?"
Bottrell outlined the details.
"So the evidence isn't conclusive then?"
"No primary evidence, only circumstantial. We suspect Druitt may had had other victims, possibly in Suffolk but there's no proof."
"And the Bristol and Somerset area, yes, I understand all that. Listen, we have a number of files relating to missing girls in our cold case division. It might be worth your while paying us a visit and trawling through the evidence. It would be impractical to send it all to you. There's too much stuff."

A Cromer Corpse

Cold case division. In his day it had been called the Special Investigations Unit. A tall red brick villa in Great George Street. But that was a long time ago.

"Where's your cold case division?"

"Same place as it always was. You'll come then?"

"I can be there tomorrow."

"Phone me on this number when you arrive. It'll be good to see you again. Catch up on old times."

Bottrell took a note of his number, then closed the phone and began eating his breakfast. Bristol 1976. The baking hot summer. Distant memories of the stifling city and long vigils in Ford Escorts. The place where he had met the first love of his life. He hadn't been back there for decades. How much of it had changed he wondered?

He cleared away the breakfast things then, picking up his pipe and jacket, made his way slowly up the track in the direction of Morton Wood. To his right he could make out the small group of volunteers working on the archaeological site, their yellow safety helmets glinting in the sun. Stopping to chat with the dig supervisor for a moment, he then walked on. Soon he was inside the great green canopy of Morton Wood where giant oaks and beeches bounded the narrow footpath. Since it was still early there was not a soul about and the wood was cloaked in a deathly silence as if the birds had altogether deserted the place. About halfway in he sat down on a fallen tree trunk and charged his pipe. Soon he found himself slipping into a nostalgic reverie about former days in Bristol. But his mood was broken by a sound from close by. At first he imagined it to be a bird, a magpie perhaps. But there it was again, this time closer. Surely it wasn't a bird but the sound of a child's voice? He sat up, alert, but there was nothing now save the silence of the wood. Maybe he had imagined the whole thing.

A Cromer Corpse

Extinguishing his pipe, he made his way back down the footpath. A slight breeze had now risen and the branches overhead swayed and rustled as he walked. When finally he cleared the trees and was back on open land he felt an inexplicable sense of release wash over him.

When he reached Morton Mere he took out his phone and rang Mel.

A Cromer Corpse

CHAPTER TWENTY TWO

Julia Stevenson had just finished drying her hair when the doorbell rang.

"Sorry to disturb you at this hour Mrs Stevenson," Grayling greeted her. "Are John and Abigail in? We need to speak to them."

"I'm due to leave for work in about half an hour and I need to drop them off to school. Can this be brief?" Her manner was brisk.

Grayling and Waverley stepped into the lounge and Mrs Stevenson left them for a moment, leaving an odour of fresh lavender behind her. Grayling sat on the leather sofa and gazed round the room. A large, crudely constructed pine bookcase stood opposite, filled with books on new age spirituality and wicca; there was an old oak table strewn with papers and magazines whilst a lap top perched precariously on a green wicker chair. He glanced at the screen: "Yahoo Instant Messenger": and beneath the legend was a short missive from someone called 'Raven' regarding moon rituals. He was interrupted by John and Abigail, the former looking even more pale and gaunt than before. His sister sat on the chair opposite and stared inscrutably at them.

"What's this about?" asked John.

"We need to check some details you gave us in your statement regarding Annie Banham," said Waverley.

"They didn't give you a statement – not a formal statement," Mrs Stevenson interjected.

"We know that, Mrs Stevenson. DC Waverley is referring to the conversation which took place when we were last here." Mrs Stevenson continued to hover.

A Cromer Corpse

"According to Susan Blight, Annie's friend, Annie used to visit the area of Morton to carry out rituals with you. Is that right?"

"Yes, sometimes we did that," John replied.

"When we questioned you last you claimed you'd met Montague Druitt on a couple of occasions when he'd attended the Moots."

"That's right."

"Yet you were also seen on a Saturday in early June coming with Anne and Druitt coming out of a café in Morton."

John looked at his sister.

"I don't remember that."

"We have here a diary Annie kept," said Waverley. "It's quite detailed about places, people she met and events. It mentions you both in connection with rituals you took part in with Druitt – in fact it mentions this seven times. The last of these took place in late June. Do you not remember that?"

John Stevenson was beginning to look uneasy.

"Why didn't you tell the police all this?" asked his mother, angrily.

"Isn't it obvious?" he blurted.

"Have you heard of an organisation called The Sons of Paracelsus?" asked Grayling.

"Yes."

"You knew Druitt was a member of that organisation?"

"He talked about it once, yes."

"Did he ever ask you both if you were interested in joining?"

"No. He told us about it once when we visited his house. He was into High Magic, the Golden Dawn, freemasonry, that kind of stuff."

"And what did he tell you about it?"

"Very little. It seemed to be a series of rituals based on the old grimoires. It wasn't really our thing. I told you, Abi and me are really into the Northern Tradition."

"Did you at any stage take part in a ritual with Druitt when Annie was present?"

"No. Monty was friendly towards Annie but it was completely innocent. He was like an uncle to her, you know, like the dad she should have had. You didn't know her dad. He was a right bastard. Beat her mum. Monty was kind to her. Considerate. Used to buy her things, made her feel good."

"And her mother knew about all this?" asked Waverley.

"She didn't tell her mum much about what she got up to. She was independent. It told you all that before."

Mrs Stevenson was looking at her watch. "Look inspector, is there anything else you need to ask? We're running late."

Grayling stood up. "No, that's all for now. Thank you for your time, Mrs Stevenson."

As he and Waverley left the room, Grayling glanced momentarily at John Stevenson. He smiled knowingly back at him.

* * *

Slowly, Bottrell made his way up Park Street, overwhelmed by the roar and stench of the Bristol traffic. Even during the short walk from Temple Meads Station he had found the city he'd once known profoundly transformed. Much of the dockside had been redeveloped and the skyline was now dotted with uncompromising skyscrapers.

However, the tall, red-bricked Georgian villas of George Street were much the same as he had seen them

A Cromer Corpse

in the '70's. The logo on the porch of No. 27 was different. Instead of "Special Investigations Unit" it now read: Avon and Somerset Police: Cold Case Unit." He pressed the intercom button, declared himself and the automatic doors admitted him into a white walled air conditioned interior. The man who approached him with outstretched arms was older, more worn, but instantly recognisable.

"Dave Thomas. I can hardly believe it. Thirty odd years, isn't it?"

"Don't remind me," replied the tall, stocky Welshman. "Where are you staying?"

"B and B off Park Street. It'll do me."

Thomas pressed the lift button. "The place is bigger of course. They've built an extension on the back where there used to be a garden. Remember?" He nodded. He had sat there with Frances, drinking coffee. "And the team is bigger – naturally. Five of us, including the two forensic experts."

The lift stopped on the second floor and they got out. Bottrell gazed at the open plan office and the forensic rooms beyond.

"This is me on the left. Make yourself at home while I grab us some coffee. Three sugars isn't it?"

"You remembered."

Thomas returned bearing two cappuchinos.

"Bit more high tech than in my day."

"Listen, John, I'm two years off retirement. I've – sorry – we've – solved nigh on eighty cold cases in the fifteen years I've been in charge. But in all that time we've never had a lead on these particular ones."

He lifted a wad of files from his in tray and placed them on the desk in front of Bottrell.

"All three were girls aged thirteen. All went missing from the Bristol area, one in '76, one in '80, the other in

A Cromer Corpse

'88. Have a look at these files, John, and tell me what they have in common."

He glanced through the material.

"As you say, all three were of the same age, - and background. All three blond, two from single parent, professional families."

"Correct. And there are other points of interest. Two of the mothers were, or had been, members of the Pagan Alliance. The third woman, Maria Caldicot, operated as a tarot reader at new age fairs in the Somerset area. The parent of the first girl who went missing in '76, is the only one we can link directly to Druitt. We know the parents attended a summer solstice festival at his house near Wells in June '76."

"This being the case The News Of The World became interested in?"

"The same. Druitt was interviewed on two occasions by our lads. He didn't deny he'd known Lindsey Rathbone – the missing girl – and her parents. The last time she was actually seen by witnesses was on the night of June 21st after the procession and bonfire. The parents had taken her back to the house where they were staying . They'd gone to a late night camp fire session in one of the adjoining fields."

"Yes, I read the news account Goodman sent me. The parents were criticised for it at the time."

"The grounds were extensively searched by local police and volunteers but Lindsey was never found."

"What about the parents?"

"Both were known drug users. The father had been done twice for possession of magic mushrooms, the woman for cannabis. They were your average hippy parents, I suppose. They'd known Druitt for a while."

Bottrell told Thomas about his discovery of Druitt's coded diaries and his theories about the use of children in magical ritual. Thomas listened intently.

A Cromer Corpse

"So you think Druitt may have groomed the girl with the compliance of the parents?"

"I think that's possible."

"Now here's something which will whet your appetite John. Maria Caldicot, the mother of the missing girl May, lived in Wells, only two miles away from Druitt's place. I interviewed the mother last week. She's now living in Barry. And guess what? She used to work for Helen Druitt at the bookshop in Wells. Small world, isn't it?"

"You think Helen and Monty were part of the set up?"

"I'm convinced the wife knew what he was up to. She may not have been involved in the rituals – or whatever they were. Here's the thing. When I pressed the mother for more information about the connection with the Druitts she became defensive."

"Helen Druitt claims she had no knowledge of Monty's rituals."

"Wonder why she would lie about that?"

Bottrell finished his coffee. "I need to look at these files in greater detail."

"Be my guest. I have a case conference in ten minutes. You must meet the team."

"Maybe later."

When Thomas had gone, Bottrell looked at the files. The second of the missing girls was called Charlotte Stoke. He stared at the photo. Like the others, she was blonde with blue eyes. She was wearing a psychedelic t shirt and round her neck was a silver pentacle. He leafed through the file. Mother a supply teacher in Bristol. Flat in Bath. The girl went missing on a Saturday in June when they were on a visit to Wells Cathedral. They'd been sitting outside a café when the mother went inside to use the loo. When she returned the daughter had disappeared. Witnesses reported seeing a tall man with beard and pony tail talking to the girl who the left with

A Cromer Corpse

him voluntarily. Could that man have been Druitt he wondered? And why would the girl have left with him like that? Surely if it had been a stranger she would have been suspicious of him? Unless he wasn't a stranger... If she knew him it would all make sense.

He began thinking about what the Stevenson boy had told Grayling. Druitt had shown an interest in the Northern Gods. If he was some sort of Odinist, might he have been obsessed with the Aryan ideology espoused by the Nazis? The fact that all three missing girls were blonde and blue eyed made him suspicious. What magical significance lay in this fact? And why had Annie been buried in an iron age barrow? Was that also a part of Druitt's ritual?

He was interrupted by Thomas. Hot and flustered, he was holding a tray with two cups of coffee.

"Thought you might need some refreshment. Conference concluded. I have something for you. Forgot to mention it earlier. You mentioned this man Piggott on the phone to me?"

"What about him?"

"When you mentioned him in connection with an organisation calling itself "The Sons of Paracelsus", I put his name on our computer. And guess what? Turns out John Piggott, aka Father Ignatio, visited Bristol in 1958. He attended an occult conference and gave a talk on The Golden Dawn. There was something of a mini-riot when a large crowd of evangelists broke into the Colston Hall and caused considerable damage. One of the protesters subsequently died. Piggott was interviewed about the incident. We then discovered he was wanted for questioning by both the FBI and the Dutch police in connection with several cases of child abduction. We have a file on him. Did you know he had connections with an organisation called the ONT?"

"The what?"

A Cromer Corpse
"The Order of The New Templars. It was a pro-Aryan group which flourished in Germany during the '30's. You'd best read the file."

A Cromer Corpse

CHAPTER TWENTY THREE

That night it began to rain. A slow, steady drizzle at first, turning the slate roof tops of the Bristol sky line a polished blue, then growing heavier, sending a waft of damp air in through the window of the small guest house where Bottrell lay sleeping.

At Haubois Lodge, Melanie also heard the rain. Unable to sleep, she had gone down to the lounge, consoling herself with a cup of drinking chocolate. She had heard it in the east: a long, sustained roll of thunder presaging the storm. When the rain began, she opened the French doors of the lounge and stood breathing in the smells of wet foliage and damp earth. The rain began to intensify its onslaught: thundering on roofs, pouring down gutters, beating at window panes. And with it came the wind, a howling dervish, beating at windows and doors as if clamouring to be admitted.

Melanie closed the doors, then, awed by its noise and intensity, returned to her bedroom where she sat listening to the crash of waves on Morton beach.

On Morton Hill the force of the rain began to turn the exposed earth around the open barrow into great sluices of mud, shifting it into the open grave. And all around it great beeches and oaks flexed and twisted with the force of the gale, shedding leaf-heavy branches onto the exposed earth, snapping the barrier tape as they fell.

When the phone rang at 5am, Grayling was already awake.

A Cromer Corpse

"Waverley here, sir. Sorry to disturb your beauty sleep."

"You didn't. And I'm far from beautiful, as you well know, Hannah .What's up?"

"You may not believe this but – "

"Try me."

"We have Michael Banham in custody."

"How come?"

"Neighbours reported a domestic at Andrea Banham's house in Earlsham. When uniformed got there, they found a man answering Michael Banham's description. The wife's also here, helping us with our enquiries. She's pretty badly beaten."

"Have you interviewed him yet?"

"No."

"Good. Keep him on ice until I get there."

* * *

By mid morning the following day the rain storm had moved away, leaving the streets of Bristol fresher than they had been for weeks. Bottrell decided to take a walk down to College Green. It had been over thirty years since he'd been in this great city and when he saw the tall tower of Bristol Cathedral and the incongruous medley of new and old houses on Park Street, a wave of nostalgia overcame him. It was a nostalgia not for the city itself but for Frances whom he had first met here so long ago.

He bought a sandwich in a small café, then made his way across the Green to the imposing public library. In his attaché case was the file Thomas had given him the previous afternoon, but he had decided he needed antique surroundings and solitude in order to absorb its

A Cromer Corpse

contents. Somehow the stark, pristine environment of the Cold Case Division made him feel ill at ease.

He climbed the marble staircase and found the ornate reference room, much as he had remembered it save that the old reading lamps had gone and the tables seemed contemporary and out of place. The reference room was quiet at this hour save for a few desultory readers and a vagrant, seeking sanctuary, who rocked in his chair on the row in front of him.

He opened the file. "CASE REPORT ON JOHN PIGGOTT, AKA FATHER IGNATIO," it read. Unconsciously, he reached into his pocket for his pipe, then remembered the smoking prohibition and cursed beneath his breath.

"John Alfred Piggott, born 1928, Quebec. Educated at Harvard University, 1948 – 1951. Operated as an occult bookseller, New York, 1952 – 1956, during which time he was a member of The Golden Dawn. In 1957, he established an occult group called "The Golden Dawn Revived" and travelled extensively both in the UK and Europe. He was greatly influenced by the writings of Peter Van Liebenfels, an Austrian occultist. Liebenfels had been a member of an organisation entitled "The Order Of The New Templars," a pro – Aryan German group founded by Matthias Lanz in 1903 and based on the Templar Knights. According to Liebenfels' theology in his book "Theo-zoology or The Electrons of The Gods," the fall of Adam denoted the racial compromise of the Aryan races due to their interbreeding with lower animal species. The consequence of this sin was the creation of several mixed races which threatened the proper authority of Aryans throughout the world. Liebenfels claimed that the "gods" or early beings had possessed extraordinary sensory organs for the reception and transmission of electrical signals. These organs allowed the gift of telepathy and complete omniscience

A Cromer Corpse

on their owners but in modern man this had atrophied into the pituitary and pineal glands because of the miscegenation of the god men with the beast men. Only a programme of segregation could restore that lost power to the Aryan race.

"Liebenfels derived the word "race" from rata, an old Norse term meaning root in order to conclude that God and race were identical. He also claimed that the Aryans were "the sons of the sun, the sons of the gods, the supreme manifestation of life." He believed that the runes were conductors of a subtle energy which fitted the universe and that they were a link between the macrocosm and the microcosm of Aryan man. 'The runes will lead the true seeker back to his cosmic homeland and provide a mystical union with God.' The lost world of Atlantis, the stone circles of Europe, the rune futharks and astrology were to Liebenfels all evidence of the former civilization of the Aryan race. In his view, magic, mystical vision and world power would all eventually be restored to the inheritors of the Aryan culture.

"In 1907 Liebenfels purchased a medieval ruin on a rock cliff above the River Danube and it was from here he set up his Ordo Novi Templi. The activities of its twenty six members included festivals which coincided with the four seasons. He created a liturgy and several elaborate ceremonies for the Order, a book of psalms and a volume of devotional pictures, all of which fused beliefs of Catholicism with the sexo-racist gnosis. The order was split into Novices (aged over 24 years and required to be more than 50 per cent racially pure) and Masters (required to possess 75 – 100 per cent racial purity). The Masters were referred to as Fraters or Fathers.

A Cromer Corpse

"During the 1950's Piggott made connections with several neo-Nazis in America who helped him to found "The Sons of Paracelsus". The name of this organisation was intended partly to deflect attention from the hidden agenda of Piggott's group, whose ideology was based almost entirely on Liebenfels' teachings about racial purity. Funded by the organisation, he and three other members embarked on a series of lectures around Europe but in both Amsterdam and England were met with hostility from anti-Nazi organisations.

"On January 6th, 1958, Piggott, then calling himself Father Ignatio, gave a lecture at the Colston Hall, Bristol. By 7pm when the meeting commenced, a large crowd of protesters had assembled outside. By 8pm police were called when the crowd burst into the hall, overturning chairs and invading the main stage. In the melee that followed, a Bristol university student, Alan Metton, was fatally stabbed. Despite extensive investigations, his attacker was never identified.

"In March 1958 Piggott was deported as an undesirable and the Sons of Paracelsus was classified by the Home Office as a dangerous cult."

Bottrell closed the file, thrust it into his attaché case, then made his way out of the library onto the Green. Finding a park bench, he sat in the sunshine. It seemed clear now that Druitt had subscribed to the Aryan fantasy formulated by Liebenfels and promulgated by Piggott. And the fact that the Home Office had banned the cult suggested they regarded it as highly dangerous. He filled his pipe and sat for some while, watching the skateboarders as they careered to and fro along the path. But his mind was miles away. He was picturing the

A Cromer Corpse

barrow on Morton Hill and its fair-haired occupant, a sacrifice to the Old Gods.

* * *

"How long have you known your husband was in the area, Mrs Banham?"

DCs Rankin and Waverley were sitting in interview room three. Opposite them, her hair bedraggled and her upper lip and left eye severely bruised, sat Andrea Banham. She had arrived in a squad car at Norwich Police HQ at ten that morning, exactly one hour before Michael Banham had been arrested in a house in Earlsham.

"I came back two nights ago to find someone had been in the house."

"You'd been burgled?"

"No. No one had broken in. That's how I knew it had to be Michael. He had a key. Someone had gone through my personal effects, taken my credit cards. Fortunately I had cash on me."

"You didn't think to phone us?"

"I wanted to see him. Sort things out."

"And you waited until the next day?"

"I waited in all day. Sat in the upstairs bedroom. You get a good view of the street from there. Then I saw him."

"You confronted him?"

"I was furious with him. He wouldn't talk to me. Refused to answer any of my questions. Wouldn't tell me where he'd been or why he'd left. All he said was he'd come back to get even with Druitt. I lost my temper. Threw something at him. That's when he attacked me and left."

A Cromer Corpse

"How did you find him?"

"I'd spotted the taxi from the upstairs window. I know the guy who runs the taxi firm. I rang him and told him what had happened. He gave me the address. Turns out he'd been living with a woman in Earlsham.

"Under an assumed name. One Colin Williams. And claiming benefit. Colin Williams died in Glasgow a year ago. Somehow your husband got hold of his ID and used it. Quite successfully it seems."

"I wish he'd never come back. I wish he were dead."

Rankin looked at the worn face of the woman sitting opposite him. Perhaps she was right. Things might just have been a whole lot simpler.

* * *

Michael Banham had already spent over an hour in interview room two and was showing signs of strain. He hadn't washed or changed his clothes now for three days, his dark hair was matted and tangled and he smelt of sweat and tobacco. To make things worse, his left cheek and eye were bruised where he had resisted arrest earlier that morning. For that he had Grayling to thank.

The door to the interview room opened and Grayling entered, holding three cups of coffee. He handed one to the uniformed PC on the door, then sat opposite Banham.

"Cigarette?"

Banham grimaced, taken aback by this apparent hospitality.

"Now, where were we? You were telling me about Monty Druitt. You said you came back to Norfolk over a month ago with a woman."

"Her name's Liz."

"Liz then. Whose parents live in Earlsham."

A Cromer Corpse

"I knew her before I left Norfolk. We've been friends a long while."

"You mean lovers."

Banham shrugged.

"She got a place at Glasgow College of Art. I decided to chuck it in with Andrea and move in with her."

"And this Liz. Is she also part of the crack scene?"

"I told you. I don't do crack any more. I cleaned up at a rehab in Scotland."

"But you were an addict when you left Norfolk in June last year. That's correct, isn't it?"

"That's true, yes. But I'm okay now. Look, you don't have any reason to keep me here. I want a solicitor."

"All in good time, Mr Banham. I need to ask you about your movements on June 21st last year first. The day your daughter went missing."

"That was the day I left for Scotland."

"What time of the day did you leave?"

"In the evening."

"The interesting this is, Mr Banham, we have the diary kept by Druitt and in it there is an entry which mentions a meeting the two of you had on June 20th. You want to tell me about that?"

"That was a business meeting."

"What kind of a business meeting?"

"I owed him money."

"And why was that?"

"I told you earlier. I had a dependency problem. Monty had connections. He and a guy called Riscorla supplied me with crack. They had a link with someone in Europe."

"We know that. We also know that Druitt had a connection with your daughter. You knew about that, didn't you?" Banham clenched his fists. "In fact he had designs on your daughter. He had a taste for young girls. Virgins, to be precise. Did you know that? You're not saying anything, Mr Banham. Why is that?"

193

A Cromer Corpse

Banham was staring fixedly at the table.

"Your wife tells us you boasted about getting even with Druitt and Riscorla," Grayling continued. "What did that mean?"

"Okay. I'll tell you. I owed Druitt a great deal of money for the crack he supplied me. When I told him I couldn't pay he said I could pay in kind. He told me I could bring him Annie. He said he wanted to use her in some ritual he was doing. He assured me no harm would come to her. What choice did I have? She arranged to go to this pop concert at Blackling Hall on the evening of June 21st. I said I'd give her a lift. Instead I took her to Druitt's place. I told her he wanted to see her and she could go to the concert later. I thought she'd be alright. I trusted him."

"And you left for Scotland when?"

"I got the coach from Norwich around 6pm."

"And when you read about Annie's disappearance in the papers why didn't you come back or at least let the police know about your suspicions?"

"How could I? I knew I'd be implicated. When I phoned Druitt he said she'd left his house and gone to the concert."

"And you *believed* him?"

"I had no idea he was a paedophile. Not then."

"He wasn't a paedophile, Mr Banham. He may well have been worse than that."

Banham put his head in his hands, then looked up at Grayling who thought how tired he looked.

"I suspected Druitt and Riscorla must have been implicated. They were close. So I persuaded Liz to come back with me and we stayed at her parents' place."

"So you paid Druitt a visit?"

Banham sighed. "Shortly after I got back, I saw Druitt's car by some sand dunes. It was pure coincidence. He was sitting there waiting for someone.

A Cromer Corpse

Boy he was surprised to see me! It was hot and he had the driver's window open. He didn't see me coming. I put my hand through the window and grabbed him by the throat. I kept squeezing his throat, telling him not to lie. I just wanted the truth. But he kept on lying. In the end I hit him."

"Hit him with what?"

"With a pair of pliers I had in my pocket. He blacked out then but when I left him he was still breathing."

"You left? Why?"

"I heard a car. Guessed it would be whoever he'd arranged to meet."

Banham drank his coffee and finished his cigarette. Outside the interview room Grayling spoke to Waverley and Rankin.

"Well?" asked Grayling. "What do forensics say?"

"Two clear prints, one on the dashboard and one on the steering wheel, both matching Banham's."

"Question is, was Banham the second person. You checked the shoe size?"

"No joy there," said Rankin. "Banham takes a whopping ten."

"And we know Druitt was drugged before he was murdered. Which rules out Banham – if his story is true. He knew Riscorla of course... Still, there's something that doesn't tally. You checked out the girl's story?"

"She backs up what Banham said. The timing matches."

"I just wonder if Evans is connected with this. Maybe Riscorla, Evans and Banham were in it together, planned the whole thing. Bring Evans in. We'll question him. See what we can get from him."

Rankin nodded.

"What about Banham?"

"We'll release him for now. But we keep tabs on him."

A Cromer Corpse

CHAPTER TWENTY FOUR

After Michael had died, she sat for long hours on the beach, watching the white – crested rollers break, listening to the cries of gulls, turning the matter over and over in her mind. Uncle had brought tragedy to her life. He had opened a portal and the darkness had spilled through, consuming her world. It was not just her parents' death which motivated her to seek revenge. There was something else too, a terrible taint of her soul which had commenced that day she had seen him in the cabin in the woods, carrying out his black rituals. From that moment onwards, he had haunted her, poisoned her every waking moment. Although it made no logical sense, she blamed him for the death of her beloved Michael. Surely, the cancer that had eaten away at him was Uncle's doing, a magic wrought not on the physical but the spiritual level. Somehow their destinies were intertwined, she knew that, every fibre in her body told her it was so, and until she rid herself of his dark spirit, she would never be free of the cloud of misery that overhung her and stained her waking moments.

One afternoon as she lay on the sands, she watched a cormorant dive into the waves, then re-emerge, a fish struggling in its beak. In that single moment she knew what she must do. She would become the huntress, adopt the guise of Diana, stalk her prey, learn to wait in the shadows until the time was right, then pounce on her victim. She would need all her cunning, all her resolve to accomplish the task, but, through patience and perseverance she would accomplish her end.

A Cromer Corpse
* * *

Bradley Evans had begun to sweat. It was hot in the interview room and, since there was no window or air conditioning to alleviate the humid air, it was unbearable. Grayling and Rankin had removed their jackets but their shirts bore wide damp patches under their armpits and in the small of their backs. Evans, a large, corpulent man, was drenched in sweat. Every few minutes he would apply a grubby handkerchief to his glistening forehead and bald pate, then shift uneasily in his seat to unstick his damp thighs from the hard plastic chair.

Grayling passed him a bottle of chilled water, then continued with the interview.

"I must ask you about the day of the Lodge meeting in Morton. Tell me about that day."

"Again?"

"Again."

"I was in the shop in the morning with Alex. In the afternoon we closed and went back to the house. I had something to eat. I showered, then went to the Lodge around 6pm. We were hoping to meet Monty there but he never showed, so Alex phoned him on his mobile but there was no reply."

"Are you sure you don't want to tell us the truth about what happened?"

Evans dabbed at his face and stared at Grayling.

"What do you mean?"

"We spoke to Alex two days ago. He told us you went to Norwich in the afternoon on the pretext of seeing a contact about an antique mirror."

"That's true…" he faltered.

"You had no alibi," Grayling persisted. "You'd arranged to meet Druitt, you wanted to have it out with him about Mike. When you got to the dunes you found him at the steering wheel, probably barely conscious.

A Cromer Corpse

You hit him, then dragged him from the car and loaded his body into the boot of another car. At some time that same afternoon you paid Riscorla to drug Druitt, then still alive, take the body on his boat and dump it at sea. That's what actually happened, isn't it?"

Evans groaned. "I knew this would happen. That's why I got Alex to cover for me. I told you, I didn't hate Monty. I could never have done that to him. The whole thing's a bloody nightmare."

"Tell me, what size shoe do you take?"

"A size 5, why?"

"A size 5 trainer print was found near the crime scene. We can also prove Riscorla used his car to transport the body. And when we test your DNA with traces found at the murder scene we can prove you murdered Druitt. Anything you'd like to tell us? Make a clean breast of it now and it will go better for you at your trial."

"I want to see my solicitor."

On the balcony outside the staff canteen Rankin and Grayling stood smoking and staring across at the orange skyline. It was nearly sunset and a dank mist had almost enveloped many of the taller buildings which made them appear like ghosts in a grey sea.

"That bit about the DNA, sir..."

"I know. I made it up. As we know, Druitt's corpse was clean of DNA. The sea water saw to it. Maybe there's a chance of a match in Riscorla's car. Who knows? Anyway, for now, the evidence we have against him is only circumstantial. Maybe we'll get lucky with the footprint."

"And if not?"

"If not, we still have probable cause. Sooner or later he'll make a confession. He's not made of strong stuff. I've applied for a search warrant. Tomorrow I want his place gone over with a fine toothcomb."

"I'll see to it."

A Cromer Corpse

"It's quite likely Evans was involved with Annie Banham's murder in my opinion. Maybe we'll find something to link him."

"By the way I've been going through Riscorla's belongings."

"And?"

"We found a photo of Helen Druitt with Riscorla. Taken in a nightclub."

"Then we get Helen Druitt in for questioning."

* * *

Bottrell took the train from Bristol to Barry. He was tired of travelling and wanted a rest from the car. The journey was an unattractive one. First through the dreary suburban outskirts of Bristol, then over the broad expanse of the Severn and finally into the industrial hinterland of South Wales where plumes of sulphurous smoke stained the skyline. "And did those feet in ancient times…" he reflected, locked in a crowded second class compartment, unable to smoke, the windows hermetically sealed.

When the train finally arrived at Barry station he was relieved and made his way briskly in the direction of Princes Street, glancing at the buildings along his route. There was evidence of Edwardian grandeur here, tall, red brick places which had once housed great department stores, now occupied by cheap discount shops and clothing firms with garish neon fascias.

"Unicorn Dreams", Maria Caldicott's new age shop, lay at the end of the long, art deco parade, its windows arrayed with crystals, angels and incense burners. Inside, a tall blonde girl in an ethnic dress greeted him.

"I phoned earlier. John Bottrell."

A Cromer Corpse

"Maria's in the back doing a tarot reading. If you'd like to wait…"

She indicated a chair. Bottrell sat, sandwiched uncomfortably between a ghastly resin statue of Diana, the many breasted one, and a selection of lurid Tarot packs. Outside, in the arcade, a man in a shabby mac begged from passers by.

Maria appeared in the doorway. Tall and gaunt, she wore a simple white cotton dress, her neck adorned with an amber necklace.

"Mr Bottrell. I got the message. Please come through. Some herb tea perhaps?"

He declined. "You wanted to ask me about May."

"That's right."

"I don't know what else I can tell really. I told the police all I knew at the time of May's disappearance."

"This is May?" He pointed to a framed photo on the table beside him. A young girl with prominent blue eyes and long blond hair stared back. She was wearing a psychedelic t shirt and a silver necklace with a pentacle. She had the same slightly far-away look her mother had. "How old was she when this was taken?"

"Fifteen. It was her first Glastonbury. She had a whale of a time. We both did, despite the awful weather! I was doing tarot from a tent in those days." She stopped in mid-reflection, her voice breaking with emotion. "Do you have children, Mr Bottrell?"

"I don't."

"Nothing ever prepares you for the loss of a child. You think that one day you'll get over it, put it behind you, but it doesn't happen, believe me."

"I understand you were working in a bookshop in Wells at the time May went missing?"

"In the summer of 1980. That's right. I saw the job advertised in The Glastonbury Times. We were living in a flat in Wells at the time and since I was short of cash…"

A Cromer Corpse

"The bookshop was run by a woman called Helen Druitt."

"That's right."

"What do you remember about her?"

"A pleasant woman. Quiet but kind. She wasn't always there of course. There were three of us in the bookshop. It was quite a popular venue. It acted as a networking place for local pagans."

"Of which you were one?"

"Naturally."

"Did you know Helen socially?"

"Not socially. She kept business and pleasure separate. She was a good employer."

"And your daughter, did she visit you at the shop?"

"Yes, sometimes. She'd sit and wait for me after school. There was a room at the back. It was all very free and easy then. Well, it was Glastonbury."

Bottrell pulled out a photo of Montague Druitt.

"Do you ever recall seeing this man?"

She stared at the photo.

"The face is familiar. Who is it?"

"It's Helen's husband, Monty Druitt."

"Now I do remember him. I saw him at a lecture he gave in the town. Helen invited us to it, that's it. Something about the Golden Dawn. After the talk he came and chatted to us for a while."

"Us? Was May with you?"

"Yes, she was. Look, what are you getting at? Is this man a suspect?"

"This man was murdered recently. We believe he may have been involved in the abduction and murder of a young girl in Norfolk. We also suspect he may have been responsible for the abduction of three other girls in the late '70's and early '80's."

Her eyes filled.

"These children. Have they ever been found?"

A Cromer Corpse

"The body of the Norfolk girl was found in a shallow grave. We don't know what happened to the others. Mrs Caldicott, were you ever invited to a festival at a place called Oxley House?"

"No, it doesn't ring any bells. Why?"

"Oxley House was where this man Druitt organised a number of pagan festivals. It was also the place where one of the girls went missing."

"When was this?"

"In 1976."

"We were living in Bath then. No I have no memory of it."

"At the meeting, did you talk to this man or did your daughter talk to him?"

"I don't recall. There were a lot of people there that evening. Some of whom I knew. I wasn't with May all of the time. Oh God, I can't believe this."

Bottrell stretched out a reassuring hand. "We can't be certain he murdered your daughter. The evidence is at best circumstantial, Mrs Caldicott."

"You know I don't think I'd have been able to cope all these years had it not been for the support of friends. Helen was good to me. She came to see me often after May disappeared. After I left Somerset and came to live here I received help from an organisation called 'Friends of the Disappeared.' They sent me money. I often wondered if Helen had anything to do with it but I was never sure. Look. I kept a few of the letters they sent me."

"Would you object if I kept this photo and these letters? They may prove useful to the investigation."

"You're welcome. Memories are all I have now."

The train back to Bristol was crowded with commuters. Bottrell sat next to a large sleeping football fan whilst opposite him two teenage girls smelling of cheap perfume giggled and swore at each other. Before he had

A Cromer Corpse

left Barry, Maria had given him a folder containing a number of photos. He leafed through them: May and her mother at Glastonbury, May sitting in a clearing in a wood, wearing a long, embroidered dress, her long blond hair plaited; May and her mother on a park bench beneath tall beech trees; May in school uniform in the garden of a large house; Mother and daughter at Stonehenge with a small group of people. He stared closely at the last photo. A tall, overweight man in a white t shirt and jeans, half concealed behind a young woman. He recognised the face at once, though it was younger. It was Bradley Evans. And there, next to him, serene and smiling, stood Helen Druitt.

A Cromer Corpse

CHAPTER TWENTY FIVE

When the train finally pulled into Temple Meads Station, Bottrell sat on a seat near the station exit and phoned Maria.

"The photo taken at Stonehenge, Maria. When was that?"

"Midsummer, 1980."

"The solstice?"

"No, before the solstice. About a week before. The place is sealed off during the actual solstice."

"There's a man in the photo standing directly behind you and May. Bradley Evans. Did you know him?"

"He was an acquaintance of Helen's. Used to supply books to the shop. He ran a publishers called Gothic Quest."

"How well did you know him?"

"He was a regular visitor. A kind man. May used to get on well with him."

"Thanks. I'll return the photos when I've had them scanned. You've been helpful."

He sat watching the ebb and flow of human kind. Then he took out his notebook and wrote:

Montague Druitt
Helen Druitt
Bradley Evans………Maria & May Caldicott

Somewhere there was a connection between all five. And that connection was Oxley House. Helen had told Grayling little about her time in Somerset and there had been nothing about her in the material Goodman had

A Cromer Corpse

sent him. Yet Maria had worked in her bookshop. And Bradley Evans knew both mother and daughter. Was Evans the procurer? Was he the man witnesses had seen talking to May outside the tea shop in Wells? And did that explain why May had left willingly? It would make sense. He took out his mobile again and phoned Grayling but there was no reply. He left a message. "Charles. John. I'll be returning to Morton tomorrow. Several things I want to discuss. I suspect that Bradley Evans and Helen Druitt may have been involved in the girls' disappearances. Maybe you can get back to me."

A young couple passed him as he spoke. The man was holding the hand of a young blond haired girl. She was wearing a short summer dress and her hair was in plaits. Bottrell thought of the girl's body on Morton Hill and the dark web of intrigue that surrounded her death. Her ritual death surely had to be the work of more than one person. And whoever had killed Druitt had known about the identity of Annie Banham's killers. One of the murderers of Duitt had to have been Riscorla. But who had been his accomplice?

* * *

Rankin had been waiting outside Grayling's office a full ten minutes before he finally arrived.

"I need to see you sir. Something's come up. I think we may have a lead."

"Come in. What's this about?"

Rankin opened a flip file and took out a small photo. It was of a woman, naked, spread-eagled on a large bed, her head beneath her hands, legs outstretched.

"It's Helen Druitt," said Rankin, misreading Grayling's silence.

"I can see that. Where did this come from?"

A Cromer Corpse

"From Riscorla's laptop. It had been a deleted file but we reclaimed it, using the software."

"And this apparently is Riscorla's bedroom."

"Quite sir. My guess is Helen Druitt and Riscorla were lovers. There's no way of telling when this was taken."

"You think they may have been confederates in Druitt's murder?"

"Possibly."

Grayling tapped his fingers on the table. "Helen Druitt had no alibi for the evening of Druitt's disappearance. Let's get her in for questioning."

* * *

May Caldicott, Lindsey Rathbone, Charlotte Stoke, Annie Banham. She kept the names in a journal by her bedside table, under lock and key. Along with the names she had pasted in newscuttings about the disappearance of each girl. In each case she had contacted the parents. She had used an assumed name of course, for she did not wish her true identity to be revealed. Her letter head bore the logo: Friends Of The Disappeared and she had opened a PO Box to prevent any chance that the parents might make a connection. Some might have thought her a voyeur, intruding on private grief, but it wasn't at all like that. She only wished to keep alive the memory of the children he had abducted and slain. She sent sums of cash to them when she could afford it to provide some comfort to their distress, though she knew it would never really compensate for their loss.

Often when alone she would take out the photos of the missing teenagers and, placing them on a small table, light a candle and pray for their souls. And when she had finished praying, she would take a wax poppet she had fashioned in his image and drive long steel pins into its

A Cromer Corpse

heart and abdomen. She cursed him then for the pain and sorrow he had brought to those parents and she wept, too, for her own loss.

* * *

When they got to 51 Cromer Road, Grayling and Rankin found it deserted, although Helen Druitt's car was still outside the garage. Grayling put his hand on the bonnet.

"Car's not been used. Curtains are drawn. Wonder if she's up." He rang the doorbell but there was no reply. "Go round the back, will you? See if she's in the kitchen."

Rankin returned in a few seconds.

"Glass in the back door's been shattered."

"Let's take a look then."

They went into the kitchen. The radio was on standby and there was a smell of toast in the air. When Grayling entered the lounge he stopped, Rankin pausing behind him. An overturned table lamp. Books scattered on the carpet. Rankin looked at Grayling.

"Reckon I should call this in, sir."

"You do that. But before you do, check the phone for voicemail."

* * *

"I see," said Grayling. Bottrell had been telling him about the photo showing May Caldicott at Stonehenge with Evans and Helen Druitt. They were standing on Morton Pier. The sun, which had blazed down all morning, had now disappeared behind a dense black cloud and there was a whiff of rain in the air.

A Cromer Corpse

"Frankly it doesn't surprise me," said Grayling. "We interviewed Evans yesterday. In fact we're still holding him. You know that alibi of his didn't pass muster?"

"I didn't."

"I forget. You've been in Bristol. The boyfriend decided he didn't want to lie for him any longer. From what you've told me, there's a possibility he was involved in the killing of Annie Banham. It turns out Helen Druitt was having an affair with Riscorla. And if Riscorla was also implicated in the girl's death, so, by association was Helen Druitt. My bet is she also knew what her husband was up to regarding the other child abductions."

"Have you questioned her again?"

"Just been up to her bungalow in Cromer Road. Found the back door forced and signs of a scuffle. Rankin's put out an alert."

"There's something else you should know. It seems the parents of all three girls in Somerset were sent money by an organisation called Friends of the Disappeared. They were anonymous donations, the only address being a PO Box in Norwich."

"So who do you think was funding them?"

"My guess? Helen Druitt. Maybe she had a guilty conscience. I also discovered something else about Druitt from his journals. Several times he refers to what he describes as a Ritual Room. Seems he used it for his magical operations. When you examined Druitt's house did you notice anything like that?"

"We didn't."

As they were speaking Rankin suddenly appeared from the corner of the street. He was walking briskly and raised a hand in greeting as he approached.

"Bad news I'm afraid sir."

"What?"

A Cromer Corpse
"Bradley Evans. Duty officer found him in his cell this morning. He's hanged himself."

* * *

She awoke some time in the early morning, just as it was getting light. She had slept badly, her mind beset with confused dreams of the great festival fires at Oxley House, of the open barrow on Morton Hill and of the murdered girl, the eye sockets empty, the flesh like yellow parchment. There were others in her dream too, faces she had long forgotten, both living and dead. She shuddered, then, sitting up in bed, opened the bedside cabinet and took out the small framed photo of Peter. It was a photo she had taken of him on one of their illicit meetings on his boat months ago. He was sitting in the small wicker chair, leaning back and smiling, a bottle of wine next to him. As she looked at the photo, tears filled her eyes. How she missed him, this tall, swarthy man with his warm eyes and soft, powerful body. Monty had been cold and detached, a man driven by compulsion, obsessed by the notion of power over others. For all his faults, Peter was kind-hearted and compassionate and when he made love to her it was with his entire body and soul.

She would never forget those afternoons she had spent on the boat, his powerful arms wrapped around her, urging her on to her ecstasy, their bodies locked like pieces of a jigsaw. Even though he was dead, she could still smell his body, see his strong back and smooth, powerful thighs. He had ridden her until she had begun to lose herself in the moment. And afterwards they had lain together in each others' arms. His flesh a blanket of warmth enveloping her, his great head and long black hair a pillow against which she slumbered.

A Cromer Corpse

She wiped her face and replacing the photo, went over to the window and stared out. Already the sky was lightening in the east and to her right the sea lay like a millpond. Far off she could hear gulls calling to each other as all around her the dawn chorus stirred. She opened the window and the cool air bathed her face. Reluctantly, she returned to her bed and lay back on the sheet, thinking.

A Cromer Corpse

CHAPTER TWENTY SIX

Killing Monty had been easier than she had thought. Peter had been resistant to the idea at first, but once she told him of what he had done to her he had changed his attitude. She had shown him the photos of the children. At first he couldn't believe what Monty had done to them but when she told him of her suspicions and showed him some of the letters the parents had sent her, seen for himself the anguish they'd endured, he began to understand just why she hated him so much.

Peter had arranged to meet Monty by the dunes to discuss the consignment of drugs from Van Verhoeven. For over a year now Peter had been addicted to cocaine and Monty had been his supplier. Now he was in debt to the tune of £40,000. Part of the deal had been that Peter would work off the debt by making regular trips to Rotterdam and stowing the drugs in the hold of his fishing vessel. With Monty out of the way the debt would be cleared. She had promised Peter that once Monty was gone they could wait for a while, then move to Spain and set up a new life together. Peter and she would take the body out to sea and dump it. Monty would simply have disappeared.

When they arrived at the dunes they were astonished to find Monty slumped over the wheel, having suffered a head injury. He was still conscious. Peter pulled him out of the driver's seat and she began to force the amobarbital pills down his throat. He gurgled and choked but she did it just the same. They pushed him into the back of Peter's car and threw a blanket over him to avoid suspicion. Then they waited till nightfall, drove down to the dock and loaded Monty onto the boat. He

A Cromer Corpse

was still alive then, his eyes opening and closing, fixing her with that cold stare she had grown accustomed to hating. For some hours she and Peter sat drinking together. Then, just before midnight, they removed his clothes and bound his legs and hands. Peter was all for ditching him over the side there and then but she had not quite finished with him. She shaved him, carved the pentagram into his flesh and did other unspeakable things to him. He hadn't expected such terrible vengeance from her. Then they both heaved the body over the side into the black waters.

* * *

Bottrell arrived back at Hautbois Lodge shortly before lunchtime. He'd dropped in briefly to see Mel at the bookshop and arranged to meet her back at the Lodge when Margaret came on duty at 1pm. He found Grimalkin waiting for him on the doorstep, demanding food. Bottrell put down his attaché case, sighed, then went into the kitchen and rummaged among the tins of cat food. Then he collected the mail from the hall mat and, pouring himself a large malt, sat down in the wicker chair. Bills, mail shots, a letter with familiar handwriting. He opened the latter. "Thought you'd like to see this article from our archives. May have a bearing on the Druitt case. Regards, Goodman. PS. You came to Bristol. Why didn't we meet?" Underneath the note was a newscutting dated February 4th, 1982. It read:
"TRAGIC CASE KILLS TWO. The parents of a twelve year old girl died in a tragic road accident just outside Wells last night. Emergency services were called to the scene in the early hours to find a mondeo ablaze. The driver of the vehicle had collided with a car travelling in the opposite direction and veered down a bank, bursting

A Cromer Corpse

into flames. The driver of the other vehicle escaped serious injury. Both the mondeo driver and its young surviving occupant were taken to the Bristol Infirmary. The driver of the mondeo who suffered only minor injuries is Montague Druitt, the celebrated West Country witch. In 1976 Mr Druitt was questioned by police over the disappearance of a young girl, Lindsey Rathbone, after a pagan festival Druitt had organised at Oxley House, near Wells. Despite extensive police investigations, Lindsey Rathbone was never found. In the last few years Mr Druitt has enjoyed a degree of unpopularity among pagan circles in the West Country. Last night he declined to be interviewed about the incident. The victims of the crash were Lucy and Sylvia James and their daughter. The family had been returning home to Glastonbury when the incident occurred. It is believed Mrs James worked for Mr Druitt at his bookshop in Wells."

Bottrell stared at the newscutting, then re-read it. Then he reached for his pipe and lit it. He went over to the French windows and opened them wide. Outside an easterly wind was blowing in from the sea. He kept thinking about that detail in the news story. Mrs James worked for Druitt at his bookshop in Wells. So too had Maria Caldicott. She also had a teenage daughter. Was that coincidence?

For some while he stood smoking, trying to piece together the sections of the jigsaw. Was Druitt solely responsible for the disappearance of the three girls in Somerset and had Helen Druitt known about what happened to them? Had she been complicit in their disappearance? And was she Riscorla's accomplice in the killing of her husband? He must have lost sense of time for when he next looked at his watch it was gone 1.30pm. It occurred to him that Mel wasn't yet back from the bookshop. Just then the phone rang.

A Cromer Corpse

"Hi John. Look. Margaret hasn't come to relieve me from the shop. I've rung both her mobile and landline but she's not responding. Maybe she's not well. Do you want to come to the shop and we'll pop into the Hare briefly? At least have a quick snack."

"Fine. See you in ten minutes."

When he got to the bookshop, Mel was just finishing serving an elderly woman.

"Oh good. John, can you get the shop keys for me? They're in a desk drawer in Margaret's office."

Bottrell went through. He pulled open the desk drawer and found the key. Just then his eye caught something. A tube of pills lodged at the back of the drawer. He took the bottle out and read the label. "Margaret Jones. To be taken twice daily after meals. Amobarbital." He re-read the label, realisation dawning. The drug that had been used on Druitt. An anti-depressant capable of immobilising a person when taken in high doses. He closed the drawer and took the keys and bottle with him.

"Mel. I want you to go to the pub. Stay there until I contact you."

"What on earth's the matter?"

"No time to explain. I'll see you later. Lock up and go to the pub. Trust me."

He made his way down past the quay, heading for the Watch House. En route he tried Grayling's number but all he got was voicemail. He left a brief message then moved onwards.

* * *

It had not been difficult to find Monty's address. She had found it using Great Aunt Mary's PC. She also discovered that, since moving to the east coast, Druitt had established for himself a reputation as a savant among pagans. Clearly the world at large knew nothing about his darker magic.

An East Anglian newspaper had shown a photo of Monty giving a talk at a Pagan Alliance convention in Kings Lynn. When she examined their website she discovered he was also to be the guest speaker at another pagan function in Norwich. This time it was the 'Real Witchcraft Festival.'

She decided to attend. The event, held in an old theatre near the centre of the city, attracted a great number of wiccans, festooned in their outfits and regalia. She sat down near the front and was soon able to catch Monty's eye. The talk was about something called 'The Sons of Paracelsus', an international pagan organisation which had its roots in the western magical tradition. She listened carefully to his oration, struck by his power and charisma but all the while she was remembering her parents and the three missing girls. At the conclusion she asked several pertinent questions. It was clear Druitt was impressed by her intelligence and knowledge. It was also clear that he did not recognise her. But then, how could he? It was twenty seven years ago when she was only fourteen and the plastic surgery she had endured had given her a different face.

After the talk Druitt went to the bar and she joined him there. They talked for a while and then exchanged addresses.

It wasn't until a month later that she contacted him. She didn't want to appear too keen. Besides, she guessed he was still married. She had applied for a job in Norwich Library and was renting a maisonette in Earlsham. It was there she met Druitt again. Before he arrived she removed all personal effects that might have enabled Druitt to establish a connection with her former life. She

A Cromer Corpse

made him a meal and they drank too much wine. Then Druitt tried to make love to her.

Prior to this she didn't know if she could go through with it. But she found the inner strength to endure it. Over the years since the accident she had developed an ability to separate her mind into two distinct parts. One part represented her secret self. The other part existed on a mundane level. If she convinced herself that the mundane level wasn't real, then she could stomach Druitt's intimacies. She had lain back on the bed and allowed him to caress her. In her mind she kept the image of her parents and of the three girls he had done to death and even at last when he had spent himself the pictures of them were still there, intact. She knew how obsessed he was with her body, that he loved the smell of her, luxuriated in the feel of her, yet none of this mattered to her. Her inner sanctuary was impregnable. She would never be his.

After this first encounter they met at pre-arranged spots in the countryside. Druitt found these sessions exciting and she too professed excitement at the risk of discovery. Then the gaps between their meetings grew shorter. She would send him lascivious text messages or voice mails to goad him into passion. She knew that by doing this sooner or later he would succumb to her.

And she was right. One evening in late November he turned up on her doorstep, announcing he had split up with his wife, declaring that he wanted her to move in with him in Morton. She told him she'd have to think about it. Inwardly, she knew she had him on the hook. A week later he pleaded with her. She relented.

It was a week after that Annie Banham went missing. She read about the case in the papers, her heart sinking. She knew instinctively it must be Monty and she was

A Cromer Corpse

convinced his wife must have known about the circumstances of the girl's disappearance.

She determined there and then to avenge herself not just for the parents' sakes but also for the sake of the disappeared ones. On the day she moved into the Watch House she found Helen outside the house. She was shouting abuse at both of them and vowing vengeance. At that moment she thought: *you do not know the meaning of vengeance. But in time you will come to understand its meaning.*

Once installed at the Watch House, she was able to monitor Druitt's every move. She read his diaries, monitored his business dealings with Van Verhoeven. And shortly after she met Peter Riscorla and was instantly attracted to him. The attraction was at first physical but there was something more to it than that. Perhaps she saw in him the father she had not known since her relationship with Michael. Riscorla showered her with gifts. He called her his princess. For the first time in years she began to feel like a complete person again and that dark, cold place within her soul began slowly to thaw. Even her thoughts of vengeance towards Druitt began to fade. So for a short while hope began to flicker.

It was about a year after she discovered Riscorla was also Helen Druitt's lover.

A Cromer Corpse

CHAPTER TWENTY SEVEN

Slowly she came to consciousness. Her head ached and her throat was dry as parchment. Though the room was in darkness, she could just make out the long altar with its black candle holders and the tall wardrobe at one end which held Monty's ritual robes. She was in the ritual room in the cellar of The Watch House.

How long she had been here she couldn't tell. The last she remembered was being in the kitchen. She'd finished breakfast and had been listening to the radio when she'd become aware of a slight movement behind her. She'd turned then but it was too late. A blow to her head, then darkness.

She tried to move her arms and feet but they were securely bound with duct tape. Bound also was her mouth. She knew it was useless to try and cry out for the room was soundproofed. It was a place which held memories for her. In this room Monty had attempted the Ritual of The Summoning, using Smith, Evans and the young girl as his participants. They had taken a cocktail of heroin and cocaine before returning to the room and had emerged three hours later, silent, faces flushed. She knew then she should have intervened, put a stop to the madness but had she done so, had she informed the police, her part in the procurement of the other young girls would have condemned her. So she maintained her silence. After that night she had assumed the girl had been taken to Amsterdam like the others, to be used in Van Verhoeven's pornographic trade. The reality of what happened to Annie Banham therefore came as a terrible shock to her.

A Cromer Corpse

Any thought that she might have remained unscathed in the affair was cast aside when she met Peter Riscorla. Desperate for money to fuel his addiction, he had begun blackmailing her. He had found out all about Van Verhoeven's filthy trade and her part in it. He had evidence to prove it. She gave him money and when the cash ran out he demanded other more physical services from her.

How she came to loathe those sessions with him. His powerful, sweating body overwhelming hers, demanding that she perform certain "pleasures" for him. So she became Riscorla's whore. The situation grew worse when she discovered purely by accident that he had developed a relationship with Margaret. Riscorla was in the habit of photographing his 'sessions' as he described them. One evening she found a photo of them in his bedside table.

The night she visited him on the boat Van Verhoeven's men had been to see him. She had stood on the quayside and waited until they had left. He had broken into Druitt's house, stolen his credit cards, milked his account dry but still he owed them money. They took what he had but gave him a deadline for the rest he owed. She found Riscorla deep in his cups and ready for female company. Plying him with more whisky, she removed her clothes and straddled him. He didn't see the knife coming. Trapped by her, he fought back but the wound in his jugular had gone too deep. She waited until he gurgled his last breath, then showered and left.

* * *

A Cromer Corpse

Bottrell looked at his watch. Fifteen minutes had passed and still no reply from Grayling. Still, he had contacted the emergency services. He was standing in the small garden at the rear of the Watch House, hidden by trees. He had figured it out. The Ritual Room must be a cellar for at the back of the house was a large trap door with a brass padlock. On arriving he had knelt down to examine it. A sliver of light was just visible from beneath and he could hear a voice moaning.

He had been wrong in his assumption about Helen Druitt. She had not been the organiser of the Disappeared Ones, that was certain. The postman at the sorting office had given him a remarkable clear account of the woman who collected the post each fortnight and it did not fit Helen Druitt's description. However, it fitted Margaret Jones like a glove.

There was a second voice now, angry and insistent. He decided he must act and hoped that back up would arrive shortly. Taking off his t shirt, he wrapped it round his left fist, then walked up to the back door and smashed the glass. He unlocked the door from the inside and opened it. The kitchen was empty but a strong smell of perfume hung on the air. In a corner of the room a radio was playing the Liebenstod from Tristan and Isolde. The irony was not lost on him.

Good. The radio may have muffled the sound of breaking glass. Must be quiet. Which way? Through the hallway. Entrance must be somewhere on the left.

He found it, a small door which appeared to be a cupboard door but wasn't. It was slightly ajar and he could step downwards. Gingerly but quietly he pushed the door open and began his descent.

Margaret Jones' face was a mask of cold fury. She stood opposite Helen Druitt, a long kitchen knife in her

A Cromer Corpse

hand. Blood was streaming from Helen's forehead and her eyes were full of fear.

"And you did nothing to stop him. Even when you knew what had had happened to those girls, what torment and abuse they must have suffered. You didn't care. You lived with him all those years, covering up for him, sharing his perversions, like some filthy whore, serving his bestial needs. Tell me, were you there when the Banham girl died? Were you present?"

She lunged forwards, ripping the tape from her lips. Helen Druitt moaned.

"I couldn't say anything. Couldn't go to the police. If you'd been in my position..."

The knife slashed at her cheek, leaving a ribbon of blood in its wake.

"Don't even try to excuse yourself. Don't even think of doing it. Monty took a long time to die. You didn't know that, did you? And that's what's going to happen to you. This is just the beginning."

"Help me!" Helen Druitt screamed. She was staring directly at Bottrell. The words had scarcely left her lips when Margaret Jones wheeled round to face him, her pale face full of anger.

"You!" she shouted.

Bottrell backed away, eyes fixed on the knife. But he wasn't quick enough. The blade caught him on the left arm and left him staggering and wincing from the sudden pain. By the time he had regained his balance, his attacker was past him, bounding up the stairs. And by the time he'd got to the kitchen the car had gone.

He went back down to the cellar, ripped a section from his t shirt and tied it torniquet fashion to his injured arm. Then he carried out some basic first aid on Helen Druitt, unbinding her and helping her to her feet. Back in the lounge he sat with her, listening to the wailing of the approaching police sirens.

A Cromer Corpse

* * *

By the time Margaret Jones' car was winched out of the waters of Morton Quay it was already too late. Evading the two police pursuit vehicles, the red car had crashed through the aluminium barriers at the end, narrowly avoiding a family of astonished onlookers. Since she hadn't been wearing a seat belt when the bonnet collided with the barriers, her body had been hurled forwards through the windscreen into the murky waters.

Bottrell sat on a bench, Melanie applying a dressing to his arm.

"You really ought to have this seen to properly," she protested.

"I'll be fine. I just need to sit and have a smoke." He got up and walked over to the barrier tape where Grayling and Waverley were overseeing the operation.

"Ah, the hero of the moment," said Grayling. "In future, John, perhaps you could just wait for back up before doing your caped crusader bit?"

"I must apologise for that. Just thought I might be saving a life."

"Which you no doubt did."

"How is she?"

"She'll survive. Some nasty facial wounding but nothing that won't mend in time. I'm glad you intervened when you did. Otherwise we'd be left with very little to go on regarding the missing teenagers."

"How far was she implicated?"

"She's already made a statement about her complicity in the girls' procurement, though she denies any part in the murder of Annie Banham. She's also confessed to the murder of Peter Riscorla. All in all, it's what you

A Cromer Corpse

might call a satisfactory result. What gave you the idea Margaret Jones had murdered Druitt?"

Bottrell told Grayling about the pills and the newscuttings from Goodman.

"When I put those two things together, plus the identification the postie gave me at the sorting office, I guessed it had to be her."

"And you were right of course. She changed her name by deed poll two years ago. She used to be one Margaret James. Of course the skin grafts and plastic surgery changed her look entirely. And with the passage of time Druitt just simply didn't recognise her."

"Sad for the parents of the missing girls."

"Maybe not quite so bad. Van Verhoeven has been arrested on the basis of the evidence Helen Druitt has provided. We may yet discover the girls' whereabouts."

"If they're still alive."

"Quite. So what are your plans now then?"

"To do nothing for a whole week."

"Lucky for some. I'll need a statement from you. Tomorrow maybe?"

Bottrell nodded and walked back to the bench where he found Mel staring out at the flat grey sea.

"Come on," he said. "Let's go to the pub. I could do with a drink."

This is the fourth novel in the John Bottrell series. Other titles are:

Stone Dead
Witch Jar
Flowers of Evil

A Cromer Corpse

Printed in Great Britain
by Amazon.co.uk, Ltd.,
Marston Gate.